MW00883107

THE BOOK OF SCHEMES: BOOK ONE

© 2017 Marcus V. Calvert

By Tales Unlimited, LLC.

For permissions, contact:
https://squareup.com/store/TANSOM.

Cover by Lincoln Adams

Edited by Ed Buchanan

ACKNOWLEDGEMENTS

I'd like to thank Ed Buchanan (my editor) for his expertise, steady support, and blunt-force candor.

I'd also like to thank Lincoln Adams (my cover artist) for his time, patience, and wicked-awesome skill.

Rose, thanks for keeping me in the game.

To everyone else who had a hand in this twisted thing being written (living or not), I thank you.

I must also tip a hat to my fellow artists and strangers-turned-fans. You truly are a hip crowd.

3. The Book Of Schemes: Book One

TABLE OF CONTENTS

A BREAK IN THE MONOTONY

Harry Thartan typed with the skilled boredom of a seasoned clerk. Alone in his red-hued cubicle, Harry paused to stretch as he reviewed the freshly completed memo. A glance down alerted him to a brand-new coffee stain on his bright yellow shirt, just above his bulging gut. Harry scratched his balding brown scalp, muttered a mild profanity, and wondered if the cleaners could get the stain out. Over the years, he had brought them many a challenge—from pasta sauce to blue ink to vomit from a cute newborn that one of the new moms showed off last Valentine's Day.

Harry found it odd that he hadn't felt hot coffee splash on him and reached for his oversized black mug. One sip of the tepid brew was enough to make him set it back on his desk with a prune-faced expression. While he didn't mind his dead-end job, Harry did mind the shoe-flavored java . . . even if it was free. As he did six minutes ago, Harry eyed his watch and realized that lunch was too many minutes away for comfort. Then he went back to work. In short order, the memo was double-checked and emailed.

His phone rang.

"Client Services," Harry began with well-rehearsed politeness, "Harry speaking. May I help you?"

"Could you come to my office for a minute?" Bill Gilleano's gravelly voice asked.

"Sure," Harry replied as he reached for a black pen and yellow legal pad. "On the way."

Ben hung up.

As Harry hung up, stood up, and headed for his boss' office, the fantasy of being fired floated through his mind. Short of the company going bankrupt, he figured getting downsized was the only chance there was of him looking for a better job. Then the logical part of his brain cut in and told him to be grateful for his tiny little niche in the Meyerkoff-Lamm corporate tree. Were he to be fired, odds were that he'd end up working three times harder just to make what he was making now. After all, everyone around him had advanced degrees and years of experience—allowing them to earn a lot more cash.

A thirty-one-year-old loser, Harry recently moved out of his parents' basement. Sadly, it wasn't his choice. Tired of Buffalo winters, Harry's folks sold the family house and headed for Phoenix to be closer to his lawyer sister and her three little brats. As he walked toward his boss' office, Harry wondered why he didn't have the same ambitions as everyone else.

He wasn't lazy or stupid. There was just nothing to compel him. He put himself through six years of college, five different majors, and never graduated. It amazed him that his parents endured his inadequacies for as long as they did.

With a sigh, Harry put his self-pity into a mental drawer and closed it as he reached Bill's office. Six times the size of Harry's cubicle, it was filled with assorted mementos that corporate-ladder-climbing managers tended to have: pictures of a sexy (younger) wife, two smiling girls, *Buffalo Bills* paraphernalia, and shelves full of colored binders. Bill sat behind his desk, a still-handsome guy in his late thirties with salt-and-pepper hair and worry lines that came from the rigors of work and family. In his hands was an olive-green folder with a very thick file inside.

Harry figured that the file belonged to the drop-dead gorgeous blonde who sat in one of the two chairs in front of Bill's desk. In her early thirties, she wore a tastefully-short black skirt and red blouse. While Harry figured that she wasn't trying to show off her figure, he kind of wished she would.

He gently knocked on the doorframe and got their attention.

"Come in," Bill gestured toward the door. Harry caught the hint and closed it. Bill always liked to discuss everything via closed doors.

"Nancy Toofe," Bill introduced with a polite grin, "this is Harry Thartan."

Nancy and Harry shook hands with equally polite smiles. Bill gestured for him to sit in the other guest chair. Harry readied his blue pen and gray notepad.

"Nancy will be taking over your slot," Bill announced with a congratulatory smile. "You'll be replacing Grace on the night shift."

Harry's jaw dropped with shocked delight. While it wasn't a big promotion, it was a serious opportunity. If he impressed Bill and his superiors, Harry might end up as management someday. But then he started to worry about Grace. Grace Parcolli was the departmental ace. She had trained Harry and carried him during those first chaotic months on the job. Still, she was forty-seven and had been working out of her little cubicle for over twenty years. While she lacked Bill's ambition, she deserved to be in his chair or higher.

"What happened to Grace?" Harry asked with a hint of curious concern.

"She transferred to Operations," Bill replied. "She just sprang it on me, all out-of-the-blue. And now she's finally management."

Harry smiled his first genuine smile of the month. He raised his legal pad and quickly scribbled a reminder to buy Grace something nice—once he cashed his next mediocre check.

"Nancy here's an executive-level temp with stellar recommendations," Bill explained.

Harry wondered if it was her brains or her legs that got Nancy this far.

Bill turned a serious gaze to Nancy.

"As of today, consider yourself on a 90-day probationary period. Pull it off and you'll become permanent."

Nancy nodded as Bill stood up, grinned Harry's way, and held out his right hand.

"Either way, congratulations Harry."

"Thank you," Harry gushed as he rose and shook his boss' hand. "I just can't believe this!"

"You've earned it," Bill smiled as he sat back down. Then his phone rang. He looked down at the caller ID, frowned, and rested his left hand on the receiver.

"I've gotta take this," Bill said with obvious irritation. "Harry? Could you give Nancy the quickie-tour and then show her to HR?"

"Sure," Harry grinned as he led Nancy out of the room and closed the door behind them.

"So," Nancy asked, "where to first?"

"My cubicle," Harry replied, his face still glowing from the great news. "Tomorrow, it'll be yours."

"You never expected to rise up?"

"God no!" Harry chuckled. "I'm what you might call 'semi-skilled labor.' Hell, I never even graduated from college!"

He headed for his cubicle, eager to move into Grace's old spot, which was slightly larger. Better still, his paycheck was about to get much larger.

"Then why did they hire you?" Nancy asked.

"Oh," Harry shrugged, "I killed thirty-one students at my college."

Nancy raised an eyebrow as she skeptically eyed Harry's coffee-stained shirt.

"Without any formal training?"

"Nope," Harry replied as he stepped into his cubicle and sat behind the desk. Nancy looked unimpressed by the size and blandness of her counterpart's workspace. Still, Harry figured that she'd turn the place into a decked-out, hip office spot inside of a week.

"Why'd you do it?"

"Voices in my head," Harry shrugged. "What impressed Meyerkoff-Lamm was that I made each murder look like an accident, suicide, or natural causes. After my second year of college, they snatched me off the street. Somehow, they figured out my methodology and wanted me for Client Services."

"That makes sense," Nancy nodded.

"How about yourself?" Harry asked.

"Femme fatale," she shrugged. "I was crossing the country, sleeping with men, and then killing them . . . slowly."

"You enjoy it that much, eh?"

"Absolutely," Nancy replied with a brief, malicious gleam in her eye. "I had one of those childhoods."

"How many kills?"

She looked up at the ceiling and ran a quick mental headcount.

"Forty . . . six? And as far as I knew, the FBI hadn't figured out that there was a serial killer involved."

"But you were leaving DNA at every crime scene, right?"

"Wrong," Nancy grinned. "You can't have a crime scene without a body. I made sure that each victim was properly disposed of. All the police ever ended up with were missing person's cases."

Harry softly applauded. Perhaps Ms. Toofe was more than just a pretty face.

"Can't stand us men, huh?"

"If it weren't for the antipsychotics," Nancy confessed with an evil smile, "I'd have lured your boss to a sleazy motel, cuffed him to the bed, tortured him for a few days, and then dissolved him in acid."

"Yeah," Harry leaned back into his chair, "if I had a dollar for every time I thought of killing Bill, I'd have my own mansion by now."

"Is Bill 'clinical,' like us?"

"Nah," Harry replied, with a hint of disappointment. "He's sane. Believe it or not, he's ex-FSB, trained to infiltrate and assassinate targets on U.S. soil. And he's killed more people than both of us put together. The company recruited him ten years back. Now he simply coordinates contract hits."

"What about Grace?"

"A mob wife-turned-sniper," Harry grinned. "After her hubby ended up on death row, she was doing freelance kills to put her three boys through college."

"Aww," Nancy happily sighed. "I always wanted kids."

"But you're afraid of having boys, eh?" Harry knowingly asked.

Nancy regarded her co-worker with increased respect and hoped that her monthly antipsychotic injections never stopped working. Otherwise, she'd kill Harry real slow: not just because he was a filthy man but also because he could read her so well.

"So, what's next?" Nancy asked with a measure of enthusiasm.

"I'll introduce you to Dr. Vance Burke, our in-house shrink."

Nancy made a face.

"I hate shrinks," Nancy said as she leaned against the cubicle's entrance. "I've never killed one though."

"Well," Harry shrugged. "Give him a chance. He's not here to cure or redeem you. Dr. Burke's only role is to make sure that you stay within acceptable boundaries. If it weren't for him, I might've gone off my meds years back."

"It does sound tempting."

"Not when you weigh your odds of success (alone) versus being backed by Meyerkoff-Lamm. They protect us, train us, and have a wonderful benefits package. The only price to pay is that we have to appear to be normal. You can't kill anyone until you've worked your way out of this cubicle."

"If you're replacing Grace, aren't you afraid of being rusty? You haven't killed anyone since you came in here."

Harry looked down at his gut and gave her a knowing grin. It pleased him to be underestimated, solely on his appearance. He wouldn't boast that he could bench 340 pounds or easily jog twelve miles.

"Let's just say that our Employee Training Department doesn't just show you how to do spreadsheets better," Harry grinned. "Over my nine years here, I've learned martial arts, languages, demolitions, toxins, industrial sabotage, and a whole lot of other fun stuff. My advice is to dig into the training programs and score well. You're charismatic enough to be out of here in way less time than I did."

"I you don't mind my asking, why'd you stay so long?" Nancy asked.

Harry paused to consider the question.

"It's kind of hard to stay focused, without the voices. They used to guide my every major decision."

"So will you still have to take your antipsychotics?"

"Afraid so," Harry grumbled. "Or else, the voices might regain control and I'd go on some unpleasant tangents. Dr. Burke kept assuring me that I'll be happier, should I ever get to kill again. Hope he's right.

Either way, I'll simply fall back on my training and do whatever the firm asks."

"And my role is to cover up your kills, right?" Nancy asked.

"Yeah," Harry nodded. "Believe me when I tell you that it's utterly vital that you leave nary a trace. We kill anyone: from cheating wives to foreign dictators . . . as long as the price is right. What makes us so successful is that no one (except our clients) knows that this multinational corporation's really a clearinghouse for killers of all stripes."

"Do I go out with you in the field?"

"Sometimes," Harry replied as he set his notepad down and stood up. "But most of the time, you'll be coordinating my alibis and dealing with any loose ends. Okay, let's be off."

"To Dr. Burke's?" Nancy frowned.

"Eventually," Harry grinned as he walked past her. "First, I want to show you the armory, the chemical weapons lab, and the cafeteria—they make the best omelets money can buy!"

VIRUSED

Halfway through an evening stroll, Corey Nymber sensed he was being followed. Short, wiry, and brown-haired, the wizard didn't look a day over twenty-six. He concealed the building tension behind a calm, average-looking street face. Without slowing his stride, Corey's hazel eyes took in the uncrowded boardwalk and didn't find anyone (or anything) of note. But, after 252 years of hard living, the wizard knew firsthand that some of the worst threats were the ones unseen.

While he prayed for an old-fashioned mugging, Nymber didn't figure that would happen. Whatever was eluding his trained eye was better than the typical neo-Jersey street scum. Even semi-retired, the wizard's list of enemies grew by the year. Nymber slowly slid both hands out of his gray leather jacket and continued along the boardwalk with a half-dozen attack spells ready. Nine paces later, he casually cast a backward glance and saw no one. As he turned back around, Nymber almost bumped into the large barrel of a D49 slivergun.

Most sliverguns fired tiny carbon shards capable of punching through people like cotton candy. This particular hand cannon had a tiny, U-shaped drum in front of the trigger guard. Nymber guessed that it could fire anywhere from 300-500 rounds, with an effective lethal range of about 900 yards. The weapon looked new and fairly expensive.

Nymber's eyes shifted from the weapon to its wielder.

She was a gorgeous brunette in a black, one-piece outfit that clung to her perfect frame like body paint. Silvery spikes extended from around her outfit's chest, waistline, and tight-fitting collar. Her black, steel-toed boots looked more utilitarian than stylish.

The wizard guessed her to be a bit north of thirty, with piercing blue eyes, short black hair, and a fair amount of muscle. A diagonal line of five ruby studs protruded from her right cheek and stopped just shy of her upper lip. Nymber didn't recognize the symbolism (if any) of the piercings, but he liked the look. What he didn't like was her cold-faced expression, which screamed "hired gunwoman."

His occult senses picked up the faintest hint of a bio-aura, which meant that she was either recently undead or a cyborg. Based on the skilled manner of her ambush (and the lack of a rotting smell), Nymber assumed that she was the latter. Her slivergun wasn't mystical, or he would've sensed it a block away. That meant she didn't know about his invulnerability to regular ammo, which merely bounced off him. Still, he chose to act calm, cool, and innocent. That way, the gun-toting beauty would be more inclined to talk rather than ruin his clothes with sliverfire.

"What should I call you, beautiful?" Nymber asked with a charming smile, as he raised his hands shoulder-high in a relaxed gesture of surrender.

"Call me Kore—with a 'K'," she replied in a low voice.

"Sorry to be concerned, 'Kore—with a K,'" he nodded toward the slivergun. "But is that thing loaded?"

"They say you're a wizard," Kore said, ignoring Nymber's wit. "One of the last. I need your help."

"Wizard?" he chuckled with a convincing smile. "You must be misinformed. I'm a magician. I only do magic tricks."

Nymber whipped out a black ace of spades. On the back of it was his contact information, with just his name and vidphone number. He always kept one up his sleeve, in case someone wanted to hire him for a lounge act, charity benefit, or the occasional freelance op.

He slowly held it out.

"My vidphone number's on the back," he added with a wink. "Perhaps, when you're unarmed and in a frisky mood, you could call me sometime."

Nymber wasn't sincere about the flirtation. As far as he was concerned, lady cyborgs were little more than wind-up toys. He preferred real women with all of their God-given bits and parts attached. About the only fake things he'd want on a woman would be lactating nanobreasts full of rum.

Neither the cyborg nor her gun moved an inch. After a few seconds, Nymber took the hint and tucked the card into his jacket.

"All right," he sighed. "Say I was a wizard. What do you want?"

"Do you know Tony Lidrane?"

"Yeah," Nymber frowned. "He runs most of the rackets in this town."

"He was downloading a standard cyberskill enhancement program into his personal brainware. During the process, something slipped into him. Like a virus."

"Then shouldn't he be calling Tech Support?" Nymber asked. "I know diddly-shit about cyberware and viruses—"

"This isn't a virus," Kore impatiently interrupted. "Viruses don't make you sprout white claws and three curved horns from your forehead."

Nymber's eyes bulged as he stepped around Kore's slivergun and got into her face.

"Did his skin change color?!"

"Coal-black," Kore nodded as she lowered her weapon, thrown off by the wizard's horrified reaction. "Then, he grew about a foot taller and started ripping his people apart—"

"Where is he?!" Nymber interrupted.

A sudden clap of distant thunder caught their attention.

Kore and Nymber both turned to face the skyline of Atlantic City. Over the rooftop of The *Lion House Casino*, the tallest building in town, a dark-grayish cloud suddenly spilled out of the clear night sky. Full of crackling purple energy, it gushed outwards in all directions like blood from a fresh wound.

Nymber's face went pale as he turned back toward Kore.

"The *Lion House*, eh?"

Kore nodded.

"What's happening to him?" Kore asked, mystified.

"Cyber-demonic possession," Nymber replied, his mind at full-throttle. "Heard about 'em. But I've never seen one up-close."

Had she not personally seen Tony Lidrane's occult transformation, she would've scoffed at the idea.

"You can fix this, right?" Kore reasoned. "Do some kind of exorcism?"

The wizard pulled out his palm-sized vidphone, trying to think of a civil reply to that ridiculously stupid idea. Besides, Tony Lidrane's soul was probably reduced to metaphysical crumbs by now.

"Normally, I'd be happy to," Nymber tensely replied as he dialed a sixteen-digit number. "The idea of Tony Lidrane owing me a favor does have its appeal. The problem here is that we're out of time."

"What do you mean?" Kore asked.

"See the purple lightning? That's not a by-product of a regular possession. He's been taken by a Drethun Queen."

"So what? We'll get whatever you need, trap him somehow, and you'll do the exorcism."

"Please stop talking," Nymber mockingly laughed as he finished dialing.

He neglected to tell her that the last time a Drethun Queen entered the mortal plane was 2133, in Geneva. Luckily, some twin druid hotties he knew were nearby and managed to reach the host before it could spawn. The battle left them both seriously injured but they were lucky enough to kill the host in time.

Only eighteen city blocks—and hundreds of lives— were lost in the mystical crossfire.

The ladies told him that the main warning signs of a Drethun Queen spawning would be a fast-moving dark cloud. Purple lightning would flash at first (like it was now). Then, the lightning would turn a deep green, which meant that her spawnlings were entering this plane of existence as free-floating spirit demons . . . looking for bodies to call home. At that point, anyone using modern tech would be possessed by her spawn and their souls quickly consumed.

Eventually, the entire planet would be covered and humanity would be overrun by Drethun spawn (who only had two horns). They'd happily slaughter the pitifully few people who hadn't been possessed, while their queen mother would cheer them on from afar. Just like that, the Earth's name would be changed to "Living Hell."

Nymber wanted to explain all of this to Kore but he really didn't have time.

The cloud would be on them in about eighteen seconds—just long enough for him to place a vidphone call and cast one spell. The number was a hard-to-find secret he had pulled from a drunken two-star general some years back. The wizard allowed himself a quick grin as the vidphone chimed twice to signify a successful connection. Had the number not been current . . .

Nymber quickly pointed at the *Lion House* and blurted out a guttural incantation.

Kore looked over at the wizard with concern as the cloud raced toward them. While purple lightning flashed along the edges of the cloud, Nymber could see a few green bursts appear over the *Lion House* for the first time. The possessions were beginning. With the spell cast, Nymber hung up his vidphone. Nervous sweat trickled down his armpits. While he was good enough to cast spells across continents, the wizard had never tried one this far before.

"So what do we do?" Kore asked.

"I'd avert my eyes if I were you," Nymber replied as he closed his own and turned away from the skyline. "This is gonna get biblical."

Kore's retinal cyberware included flash-suppression implants, so she chose to watch the show. Four seconds later, a sudden lance of fiery-white energy punched through the heavens and struck the *Lion House* with dead-on precision. A keening wail could be heard for miles around, which put a hopeful smile on the wizard's averted face. Abruptly, the energy pulse stopped. When it did, the mystical cloud withdrew back toward the disintegrating structure, lightning and all.

The booming sound of the implosion reached the distant pair.

After a few seconds, Nymber turned around and cautiously opened his eyes. The cloud had completely withdrawn into the blast site and dissipated. All that remained was a massive, smoking crater where three hundred stories of glass and megasteel used to be.

Nymber gave a low whistle as he took in his handiwork.

"What did you do?!" Kore exclaimed.

"Mystically hacked into an orbital weapons platform," Nymber replied as he pulled out a pack of tobacco-free cigarettes and slipped one into his mouth. The wizard then lifted his left pinky finger to it and a thin blue flame erupted. He gave her a satisfied smile as he lit up.

"Nice shot, huh?" he asked before blowing out the flame.

Kore jammed her slivergun's barrel right between the wizard's eyes.

"You killed him!"

"Noo," Nymber corrected her, "I killed thousands of people *and him*. All of 'em were already doomed.

The best I could do was save the world—and our sorry asses—as well."

Nymber took a long drag of his cigarette, bothered by Kore's stewing anger.

"Why are you bitching anyway? I'm sure some other mob boss will be more than happy to hire a gal with such a huge pair of—"

"He was my father!" Kore growled.

"Oy," Nymber exhaled with rolled eyes as he muttered a quick spell.

Kore froze in her tracks, as if hypnotized, while Nymber gently pulled the slivergun out of her hand. Then he walked over to a trash bin and dropped it in. With the cigarette still in his mouth, the wizard cast another spell, one he reserved for his mortal ex-wives.

After a few seconds, the cyborg blinked and looked around, confused.

"You okay, ma'am?" Nymber asked with a pleasant smile.

She swayed a bit but nodded.

"I'm fine," Kore replied, now with all of her personal life memories wiped clean. "Where am I?"

"Atlantic City," Nymber replied as he nodded farewell, turned, and walked off.

"Oh," the cyborg nodded as she turned to observe the glow from the fiery destruction Nymber had just unleashed. "Um . . . is the city supposed to be on fire like that?"

The wizard didn't answer.

After a few more seconds, Kore turned around to repeat her question, only to find him gone.

THE SEVEN DEADLY STYLISTS

Rita Kolansky strolled toward a busy intersection, stopped, and waited for the traffic light to change. The tall runway model's long red hair was lightly blown about by a soft summer breeze under a clear, sunny sky. Still beautiful enough to turn heads, her lovely azure eyes glanced down at the Cartier watch on her left wrist. As the light changed, Rita's red Prada heels made hardly a sound as she gracefully strolled along the crosswalk. The model almost felt like she was on display in the raspberry-hued summer dress, which she actually modeled five years ago. Its silk reminded her of better, younger days, when she was in high demand and updating her wardrobe on a monthly basis.

But time had stolen her modeling spark.

In the lifespan of runway models, Rita was in the "out-to-pasture" age of thirty-seven. No amount of surgery could delay the inevitable signs of aging—either on her face or on her soul. The flow of modeling jobs had been reduced to a trickle and her lavish lifestyle faded. On top of that, she was too independent and short-tempered to marry a wealthy man and retire. Thus, Rita came here at the guidance of an old colleague who once needed "special assistance" with her post-modeling life as well.

Rita paused outside of *Perfection's Edge* and regarded the two-story brick building. Once a bank, it shut down during the savings and loan debacle of the early '90's. A few years later, the renovated building's ground level was turned into an overpriced hair salon. Located just outside of Boston's business district, Rita heard that it attracted a lot of the white-collar corporate types.

While the building looked harmless enough, something about it irked her. More so was the vague promise her friend made; that the owners of a hair salon could revive her modeling career . . . for a price. The idea of paying a "price" amused Rita, seeing as she had nothing to lose. With that sad realization, her hesitation went away.

Rita opened the door and allowed it to close behind her as she looked around. While the brick building looked plain on the outside, it was elegant within. The floors and ceilings were dark green marble. Mirrors were strategically placed, as were newer abstract portraits. Something of an art lover, she looked over the paintings . . . only to realize that these were the original works. Rita figured that the owner(s) might've put more money into interior design than the building was worth.

The stylists were all dressed in crimson uniforms. From the look of things, they were very busy. All fourteen stylist chairs were filled, with ten more customers patiently waiting their turn. Some read the salon's trendy stash of current magazines. Others watched the news from a large, flat-screen TV in a corner of the room.

Most of the gender-mixed clientele were professionally-dressed and upper-middle class. Unless a haircut required a second mortgage, Rita figured that *Perfection's Edge* had to be more than just an upscale beauty salon.

"May I help you?" A cute young stylist asked, as she deftly manipulated her female customer's drying black hair.

"Yes," Rita replied as she pulled a black card from her purse and handed it over. The stylist's middle-aged customer saw nothing but a blank black card. The stylist, however, saw the word *VANITY* upon it in fancy gold lettering—as did Rita.

"He's in the basement," the stylist said as she nodded toward a closed door that read EMPLOYEES ONLY.

"Thanks," Rita nervously smiled as she went through the door and down a flight of well-lit stairs. The stairs descended three continuous stories, without any landings. Halfway down, the fluorescent lighting had noticeably dimmed. She felt as if she were heading into a bomb shelter instead of a basement.

At the bottom, Rita found herself in a long, narrow basement lined with brick walls and cheap linoleum floor tiles. More fluorescent ceiling lights illuminated the room. Along the far-left side were seven furnished and occupied desks, each set against the wall. Beyond the desks was a plain-looking exit door.

Each desk had a guest chair positioned next to it.

The first desk was occupied by an older, plain-faced Asian woman in her apparent mid-fifties. Expensively-dressed and adorned in fancy jewelry, she reclined in a plain chair and was listening to her messages. In her right hand was a sleek cell phone. In her left was a gold coin, which she deftly maneuvered between her manicured fingers. She noticed Rita and gave her a polite nod.

As the model passed her by, she noticed a fancy nameplate on the woman's desk that simply read *GREED*. Rita paused for a moment, opened her mouth to ask about the nameplate, but then thought better of it. *If these people want to go by aliases,* Rita thought, *that's none of my business.*

She moved onward.

At the second desk, Rita passed a fat, unkempt man surfing through fantasy football sites on his PC as he absent-mindedly waved off some gnats. His work area was such a food-cluttered pigsty that it attracted a menagerie of ants, roaches, maggots, and gnats. His sweat-stained white shirt strained to keep his enormous gut from pouring over his food-stained pants. The stench he emitted was ten times worse than anything she'd ever smelled in her life. His nameplate read *SLOTH*. As she passed, he grinned at her with yellowed teeth.

Rita involuntarily cringed.

The third desk's nameplate read *ENVY* and was occupied by a bratty-looking teenage girl with metal braces and excessive makeup. Dressed in a black skirt, black turtleneck, and matching boots, Envy regarded Rita with a strange smile before she went back to perusing a stack of manila files.

Wrath, a thin man of modest height, a balding head, and deeply reddened face, was in the middle of an argument. Rita noticed that his gray trousers, plain white shirt, and black suspenders were all designer quality. He was shouting in Italian and completely ignored her as she passed. A wave of anger flashed through her as she moved passed him.

Lust was a well-toned Latino with a bad comb-over who leaned back in his chair and regarded her with a horny smile. Four of his front teeth were gold. She pegged him to be a bit south of forty, with penetrating black eyes. His purple zoot suit reminded her of a stereotypical pimp costume (minus the "pimp hat"). Rita noticed a porn site on his computer as she passed.

She reached Pride's desk and the handsome mid-50's fellow who occupied it. His feet were propped up on the desk as he tapped a pen upon a blank notepad. He patiently held a phone at his ear—clearly on-hold. Everything about him looked perfect: from his neat desk, gleaming black leather shoes, immaculate dark-gray suit, and even the dyed-black hairs on his thick head of hair. Pride gave her an appraising glance and then flashed her a perfect smile.

Rita looked past Pride and realized that Vanity was even better-looking. With a trimmed swimmer's physique and blonde curls, Vanity looked to be in his late twenties. He wore an all-white Armani suit, blue shirt, and a pair of black diamond earrings in each ear. For a half-second, she was attracted to him. Then she spotted the stack of gay-oriented magazines on his desk.

"May I help you?" Vanity asked with a high-pitched voice.

"Yes," Rita replied with a hint of disappointment as she handed him the black card. "I understand that you help people with their problems?"

"Absolutely," he replied with an effeminate wave of his hand. "Have a seat."

Rita sat as he returned the card, which she slipped back into her purse.

"What can I do for you?"

"I'm having trouble finding modeling jobs," Rita explained. "My friend, Grace Westerly, said that you could—maybe—help me get back into the field. But she was vague on exactly how you could do that."

"Yet you came here anyway," Vanity sympathetically reasoned. "Things that bad?"

Rita nodded with embarrassment. What little money she had saved/invested over the years was all but gone. She was in debt up to her eyeballs. To top it off, her loft was two months away from foreclosure.

"Would you like your youth back?"

"Anyone would," Rita lightly joked. "But you can't fight Time."

"I'm serious," Vanity replied as he reached into his desk and pulled out an ovular, antique mirror.

He handed it to Rita, who gasped as she gazed at it and caught a reflection of her younger self—when she was about sixteen. The model grinned as she thought back to those times. Her career was just starting to roll.

The parties, the men, and the money—it was all too easy. But then her mind snapped back to the reality and the impossibility of this.

"How did you—?"

"Don't worry about the pesky details," Vanity interrupted with a grin. "Do you want to be young again or not?"

"Hell yes!" Rita said with a smile.

"Interesting choice of words," Vanity replied as he produced a contract and an old-fashioned fountain pen.

Rita's quick mind connected the dots . . . and she laughed. Her melodic guffaw made the other partners turn and regard her with varying expressions. Vanity glanced over at them and shrugged. Then he regarded his prospective client.

"This arrangement is very real," Vanity insisted with a serious edge in his tone. "I'm offering you twenty-one years of youth, in exchange for your soul."

"I know," Rita said through her laughter as her youthful reflection laughed with her. "You can't fake that!"

Vanity regarded the mirror, now even more thrown-off.

"You expect me to toss out my immortal soul for only—and I repeat, only—twenty-one years of youth?! Are you nuts?! That's a shit deal and you know it!"

The physical manifestation of Vanity leaned back into his chair with a satisfied grin. It had been four years since one of his clients had the stones to haggle.

"Your friend, Grace, thought it was a good deal."

Rita frowned with curiosity.

Grace wasn't younger or better looking. In fact, the aging model had put on thirty pounds of "ice cream thighs" since she quit modeling, some ten years ago. Grace was lucky enough to marry a middle-aged dot-com billionaire, have a few kids, and enjoy spending his considerable wealth. As far as Rita was concerned, Grace had the good life.

"What did she sell her soul for?" she asked.

"Wealth, children, a controllable husband, and a long life that was free of disease," Vanity replied.

"She cut that deal with you?"

"Not just with me," Vanity replied, pleased that Rita was more than just a pretty face. "Greed, Pride, and Sloth had a hand in the negotiations as well."

Rita looked over at the other associates, who had returned to their various activities.

"She still got a shit-deal," Rita muttered. "When she dies, Grace is going to burn in Hell."

"Maybe you can strike a better bargain," Vanity purred. "Think of it, Rita: anything you could possibly wish for could be yours."

Rita shook her head, rose to her feet, and headed for the exit door.

She wasn't a saint. In fact, she was quite the bitch. Her scorecard of deeds was a mixed bag of sins and kind acts. Through her early mid-life crisis, the model had never much pondered the existence of Hell. But now that she knew that it was real, the thought disturbed her.

Rita reached for the door when it hit her.

"Grace sent me to you," she whispered, more to herself, as she turned back to face Vanity. "Why?"

"Well," Pride cut in, with a deep and elegant voice. "About five months after signing her soul away, Grace came back and signed an addendum."

Rita paused to weigh Pride's words. Then her face slowly turned red.

"Let me guess: Grace sends you X number of clients and the bitch gets her soul back?!"

"Correct," Pride replied with a proud nod. "I negotiated the terms myself."

"How many souls did she have to send your way?"

"100 souls within ten years of signing," Vanity chimed in. "Potentially, you're the 90th client."

Tears of rage began to appear in Rita's eyes as she reached into her purse and tossed Vanity's card to the floor. Then she eyed the exit door, wondering where it led. Hell, perhaps? Not in the mood to find out, she turned toward the stairwell.

"If I had a dick, I'd piss on both of you!" Rita yelled as she stormed past Vanity.

Still on the phone, Wrath glanced over at her as she passed and smiled with satisfaction. Rita continued toward the stairs.

"Why the anger?" Greed asked with a soft, tempting voice. "100 successful referrals and you could regain both your youth and your soul with the stroke of a pen."

Rita stopped at the foot of the stairs and gave the Deadly Sin a scornful grin.

"Like God would want me after something like that," she spat.

Without another word, the aging model turned and stormed up the stairs . . . leaving all types of sin behind her.

EXECUTIONER'S LICENSE

Kurt Ullerbach waited in the License Bureau's ridiculously-long line. Tall, brutish, and intimidating, the serial killer's long black hair matched his biker attire. As he watched the Mets lose to the Reds on his holowatch, Kurt cursed himself for being so late.

Last night's storm, however, shut off his alarm clocks, causing him to oversleep. Then, his victim managed to (somehow) pull herself off the double meat hooks he had left her on while he was in dreamland.

The silly blonde tracked blood all over his new carpet as she tried to crawl for the kitchen door. Luckily, Columbus (his pet terrier) was a barker.

The double-whammy of an escaping victim and losing two good hours of waking time didn't leave Kurt in a great mood. He beat his "guest" unconscious, hogtied her in the basement, and then jumped into the shower. Once he finished here, he'd go home and turn her into fertilizer for his garden. With luck, the spunky victim would add some plumpness to his tomatoes.

So far, he had waited through a cyber-rodeo, an hour of CNN, and the whole Mets-Reds game. Hundreds of people were ahead of him. Hundreds more behind. Only three employees were on duty. Due to budget cuts, this License Bureau was only one of eight in the entire state of Maine. Kurt channel-surfed through cable stations, saw nothing else of interest, and then set his holowatch to passive mode. As the line moved with agonizing slowness, the murderer wished he had brought a meal pill with him.

Two hours later, Kurt ended up at the front of the line. In spite of his aching back and feet, he felt somewhat triumphant to have endured the wait yet again. The pudgy woman in front of him had just gotten her Drunk Driver's License renewed (a relatively quick process). An effeminate gentleman, whose nametag read "Dennis," waved Kurt over.

"Good morning," the man greeted.

Kurt merely nodded and pulled out his driver's license. He handed it over to Dennis, who ignored the dried blood and bite marks on its surface.

"Need my Murderer's License renewed," Kurt muttered in a deep voice.

Dennis ran it under a scanner and raised an eyebrow.

"Wow! You've beat quota five times."

"I know," Kurt replied, somewhat irritated.
"Getting this thing renewed's starting to get expensive."
"I imagine," Dennis replied with a wide smile.

The bureaucrat started to enter a string of commands into his holoterminal, paused, and then regarded Kurt for a sympathetic moment.

"You didn't get the notice on the new Executioner's License, did you?"

Kurt raised an eyebrow, as if someone had just offered him a chance to kill a bunch of cheery, off-key Christmas carolers.

"What's that?" Kurt asked.

"Unlimited kills per year—as long as you target people on a specific list. But don't worry. The list has thousands of people on it and they're all within easy driving distance."

The thought of unlimited kill numbers gave Kurt an instant erection.

"How much?!" The killer asked, his excitement scaring the woman behind him, who simply wanted her driver's license renewed.

"A few hundred credits more than the Murderer's License," Dennis shrugged as he handed Kurt a holodisc. "The information's all here. Read it over, fill out the application, and you can have it processed in five minutes."

The murderer turned, regarded the super-long line behind him, and sighed.

"A good killer has patience," his mom always told him.

With a grudging smile, Kurt accepted the holodisc and found an empty plastic chair. Then he sat down and tapped the CD-shaped device, which activated and released a holoimage of a well-dressed female speaker. Her speech laid out the one-year duration of the Executioner's License, which would allow him to kill anyone within the city's Criminal License Database. Thus, anyone with a Pimp's License, Abusive Parent's License, or even a Jaywalker's License was fair game. There were only two snags.

One: he couldn't just kill anyone who bothered him anymore, or the police would have to investigate. Kurt knew he'd miss the freedom and flexibility of slaughtering folks for the most whimsical of reasons. With a Murder's License, he could kill fifty people per year, leave his license number on the corpse, and the police would simply log the kill.

Its only real flaw was the quota limit. If he exceeded his fifty-person quota, Kurt would have to renew. If he failed to renew, then the police would arrest him and an underpaid jury of judges would sentence him to death row in thirty minutes or less.

The second snag of the Executioner's License was that applicants ended up in a special slot on the database. If Executioner A was killed by Executioner B, then Executioner B's license would be extended three months . . . at no extra charge. Thus, Kurt could be stalked and killed by fellow Executioners—not that he was afraid of such things. He would take the necessary precautions. Besides, he could probably have some fun killing killers, while saving himself a bundle on fees.

So, he filled out the application, went to a Chinese restaurant, and had a nice lunch. Then Kurt relieved his bladder and swallowed some painkillers before walking to the end of the License Bureau's half-mile-long line. Luckily, there was a Dirty Harry film marathon on his holowatch.

Seven hours later, Kurt ended up in front of Dennis again.

"All set?"

"I hope so," Kurt wearily replied as he handed the holodisc over.

Dennis slid it into his holoterminal and grinned.

"Everything looks to be in order," Dennis replied. "That'll be 6,000 credits."

Kurt pulled out his wallet, fished out his cred card, and handed it over. Dennis processed the order and handed back the cred card with a paper receipt.

"Thanks and have a wonderful day," Dennis chimed.

"You too," Kurt replied, wondering if Dennis was in the database. If so, he'd have to pay the cheery bastard a visit with his favorite bone saw.

Kurt headed for his Harley hovercycle, knowing that the first thing he'd do is turn on his PC and see who was in the database. Odds were that his victim list would run into the hundreds by Christmas. As he pressed his thumb to the ignition sensor, the hovercycle exploded with only a mild shockwave and not much of a fireball.

Folks in line didn't even bat an eyelash as flaming bits of Kurt landed nearby. They weren't going to lose their place in that goddamned line—no matter what. From behind his workstation, Dennis grinned as he waved over someone for a Tax Evader's license.

He loved dealing with fellow Murderers.

Of course, he also had a Con Artist's License, which allowed Dennis to con Kurt out of a cool six grand. His legitimate wage wasn't nearly enough to maintain his six different licenses: Con Artist, Murderer, Drug Abuser, Wife Beater, Animal Abuser, and Arsonist. Thus, he'd cook up phony scams like the Executioner's License. The somewhat-unstable Murderers usually fell for that one.

Dennis would give them the fake holodisc to get them hooked, knowing that they'd be too impulsive to take it home and verify its authenticity. Then, while they waited in line the second time around, he'd simply take a break and slip a vibration bomb under the sucker's vehicle. The lowly bureaucrat/criminal chuckled as he processed the Tax Evader's request form.

As if Congress would ever allow an Executioner's License!

They'd all be dead in a week.

PATIENCE

Under a late-evening downpour, U.S. Marshal Christopher Ments rode up to the secluded hunting lodge of Emmet Bluss. In his late thirties, the tall, thin lawman had a weathered face which tragedy and hard living had given him. Aside from a loaded gun belt, he wore dark-hued clothing, riding boots, and a wide-brimmed black hat.

The chilly rain didn't distract Ments from his aching left thigh as he guided his brown mare toward the two-story, brick-and-wood structure. After pausing to admire the lodge's craftsmanship, he saw firelight through the front window. While he couldn't see Bluss, the marshal knew he was there.

Ments' old thigh wound made him wince as he dismounted and gently took the reins in his wet, calloused hands. Behind the lodge was a small stable, wherein he walked his mount. Two stallions nervously regarded Ments as he approached. Once his own horse was hitched, Ments headed for the lodge's front door.

The dogs barked long before Ments stepped onto the front porch. The lawman politely knocked and waited with his arms folded. He knew about Lee and Grant, Bluss' prized hunting hounds. Named after the two Civil War generals, the dogs were meant to be ironic.

After all, someone needed to repair war-ravaged railroad tracks. Bluss had the political connections, manpower, and supplies to profit off both sides without being charged with treason. When the war ended, his railroad interests expanded westward. In time, Emmet Bluss became one of the most powerful men in America.

Aside from the dogs, Ments knew that Bluss wouldn't be protected—not tonight. While his servants stocked and prepared the place for him, the tycoon preferred to stay at the lodge alone. He waited as Bluss' heavy footfalls came closer and closer. The dogs' barking abruptly ceased. Emmet Bluss opened the door and looked up at the lawman's badge and then his face. In his early fifties, the businessman wore expensive leisure attire and brown leather slippers on his feet.

Short and pudgy, Bluss wondered what the hell a U.S. Marshal was doing on his front porch. Ments evenly stared at the gray-haired man in silence. Just as Bluss opened his mouth to speak, the Marshal went for the Colt Peacemaker on his gun belt.

The six-shooter barked twice.

Bluss staggered back with a yelp of fear as Grant and Lee hit the wooden floor—each with a bullet through the head. Ments scowled as he entered and slammed the door closed behind him.

"W-Who are you?!" Bluss asked with a frightened Tennessee accent.

"U.S. Marshal Christopher Ments," he replied, the pistol firmly gripped with his right hand. Ments took off his rain-soaked hat with his left and shook it off over Grant's corpse. "Sorry about your dogs. But I wanted your full and undivided attention."

"You've got it, Marshal," Bluss gasped.

Ments gave him a dark grin and glanced over at the roaring fireplace and lavish furnishings near it. Then he gestured for Bluss to take a seat. The tycoon stepped over Lee and then raised his hands as Ments guided him toward a comfortable-looking brown sofa.

"Mr. Bluss, you're about to have a very long night."

"What do you want?" Bluss asked as he sat down, hands still in the air.

The poor bastard's reaction made him look pathetic in Ments' eyes. The lawman put his hat back on and resisted the urge to empty his gun into Bluss's face. He needed to be sure—to erase all doubts about the man's guilt.

"For one thing, I'd like you to put your hands down," Ments began. "I probably won't have to kill you tonight."

Bluss slowly put his hands down. Ments spotted a wooden rocking chair. The lawman used his free hand to drag it along the floor until it was positioned directly across from Bluss. With only a few feet between them, Ments sat down and gently rocked back-and-forth.

After a few moments of contented silence, he uncocked the pistol, yet kept it pointed at Bluss.

"Right," sighed the lawman. "I'm here to tell you a little story. Once I'm finished, I plan to leave you alive and unharmed. Do you understand?"

"Yessir," Bluss replied with a tremor in his voice.

"Glad to hear. Now, this story begins about . . . three years ago. There used to be a little mining town called Deepers Ridge."

Bluss visibly shuddered at the mention of the ghost town. Ments saw it as a clear admission of guilt.

"You must've been the one who got away," Bluss whispered. "She always wondered what happened to you."

Ments fought the urge to beat the smaller man to death with his bare hands. Instead, he swallowed hard and forced a smile.

"Honestly, Mr. Bluss, you had a brilliant thing going. Most land-snatching bastards would've sent gunmen to scare farmers off their land. The problem with that way of doing things is that everyone knows who's behind it."

Bluss nervously ran a hand through his hair.

"But you took the indirect route," Ments continued. "You actually put together the Haig Gang. Clever move."

Bluss' thoughts briefly caressed the memory of his dead sister. Victoria Haig was the union of his father and some whore from Kansas City. His father told him about his half-sister on his deathbed. Raised as an only child, Bluss was curious enough about Victoria to seek her out during the war.

Back then, she was married to a Confederate major with a child on the way. Then her husband died at Antietam. When Victoria heard of his death, she miscarried.

Her sanity died soon after.

Victoria's hatred of the Union made her join up as an assassin. During the latter years of the war, the Confederacy needed all of the help it could get. So, they simply gave her a list of seventeen mid-level Union officers and let her loose. By the end of the war, every one of them was dead. She'd use her looks and her wits to get close. Then, she'd use poison, guns, and blades to finish them off.

By war's end, Victoria had a large price on her head. When Bluss heard of her plight, he decided that it was time to meet his younger sibling. He hired bounty hunters to track her down with a simple message: to contact him. Victoria wasn't easy to find. In fact, she was so fast with a gun that some of his messengers died from it. Eventually, she got the invitation and met him at his California estate.

She stayed there while Bluss made arrangements to send her abroad. As they bonded, Victoria came to learn of her brother's problems. The railroad boom had become ferociously competitive. Even with his vast gains, Bluss was afraid that his company would be swallowed up by his competitors. Victoria told him not to worry. She offered to help Bluss expand his holdings, in exchange for his silent protection from the hangman's noose.

His thoughts returned to Ments as the lawman spoke.

"Whenever you wanted to run your railroad through someone's land, you'd point and she'd shoot. Everyone else thought that they were plain ol' murderers, bank robbers, and cattle rustlers. But they only killed certain people—mainly the folks who owned the land that you wanted. Business was booming . . . at first."

"Then, one day, she went too far," Bluss sadly smiled. "Deepers Ridge: a dying little mining town with a prime location for a railroad spur."

"We didn't see you coming, Mr. Bluss," Ments admitted. "As you know, the Haig Gang simply showed up one fine Sunday evening. They robbed the bank, torched most of the town, killed the sheriff, and fled. Once we put the fires out, the mayor deputized enough of us to form a posse. Then, we went after her."

From what Bluss heard, the Haig Gang figured they'd be followed. When the posse stopped for the night, Victoria circled about and led an ambush on their campsite. The Haig Gang gunned down the posse without mercy. At first, the bandits thought they killed them all. But then they found a blood trail the morning after, tracked it for a few miles, and lost it at a nearby stream.

Ments' mind briefly relived the agony of how he had staggered along with a bullet in his left thigh. He passed out on a road and was found by a stage coach an hour later. By the time Christopher Ments made it back to Deepers Ridge, he was about the only man left.

"Were you a lawman back then?"

"Nope," Ments grinned. "But my pappy was. He taught me a few tricks of the trade when I was growing up. Disappointed him greatly when I didn't follow in his footsteps."

"Ah," Bluss replied.

"No, I ran one of the town's two hotels," Ments explained, showing off his wedding band. "Your sister's gang sent it up in flames—along with my wife and two boys."

Bluss fought the inclination to offer condolences, fully aware that such words would only provoke the lawman. Nor did he think that Ments would take a bribe. As he eyed the restrained rage within Ments' eyes, Bluss decided not to push his dwindling luck.

"Once I healed up, I became the new town sheriff. But by that time, most of the townsfolk had chosen to leave. Between the dried-up mine, the fires, and the lack of able-bodied menfolk, one couldn't be too surprised. That's when I decided to look up your sister."

"So you killed her?" Bluss quietly asked, surprised to find his fear suddenly mixed with some newfound anger.

Ments nodded.

After Deepers Ridge, the bounty on the Haig Gang increased tenfold. Bluss had gotten word to Victoria that she needed to break up her gang and head for Mexico. Whether she had received his message or not remained a mystery. For, about two years after the events at

Deepers Ridge, Victoria had been shot in her right kneecap and then chained to the caboose of a passenger train.

The female outlaw was dragged over some fifty-eight miles of track before a passenger discovered her mangled corpse. Since his sister was a wanted fugitive, Bluss opted to leave her murder both unsolved and unavenged.

"And her gang? That was you as well?"

"Yep," Ments replied. "I gave three to the hangman and killed the other nine. Of the three I brought in, Frank Pike was the one who told me about you. He and your sister were close. She confided in him. When I found him, Pike figured that bit of information would save his neck."

"Guess he was wrong," Bluss replied. He had read about Frank Pike's execution a few weeks ago. "Why didn't you have me arrested? Pike could've testified against me."

"Thought about it," Ments admitted. "But then I realized that you'd either have Pike killed before the trial, bribe the judge, or leave the country with a few bags of gold to keep you warm at night."

Bluss realized that he'd have tried all three options, just to stay alive and free.

"No, Mr. Bluss, you needed a different kind of justice: the kind which requires patience."

Feeling sweat begin to form, Bluss wished for a cigar. A good cigar always soothed his nerves.

"What do you . . . What do you have in mind?" Bluss managed.

"Some of the older orphans from Deepers Ridge were real eager to avenge their dead kinfolk," Ments explained. "They had already learned how to shoot and track. Their mothers sent 'em to me, while I was tracking down the last members of the Haig Gang. I took 'em under my wing and taught 'em everything I knew. They were really helpful, Mr. Bluss. And when I told them that you were involved, they begged me to save you for last."

"And you agreed?" Bluss frowned.

Ments grinned as he took off his badge and slipped it into his shirt pocket. Two gunshots cracked in the distant night, followed by the neighing of his Ments' mare. Bluss jumped to his feet in surprise.

"That would be your two horses getting shot," the lawman calmly replied, gesturing for Bluss to rise.

"What are you playing at?!" Bluss asked, half-frantic as he stood up.

Ments admired Bluss' slippers, wondering how long they'd stay on his feet.

"My young 'helpers' are going to give you a one-hour head-start," Ments told him. "Then they're going to hunt you down like an animal. And if they catch you, Mr. Bluss, they will skin you like a deer. Trust me: I taught 'em how."

"But you can't—"

"If you make it to town," Ments interrupted, "you live and this thing ends."

While the lawman's words rang true, Bluss didn't believe them. Enjoying the warmth of the fireplace, Ments holstered his weapon. Then he casually drew his dad's silver pocket watch from within his coat and flicked it open. After a quick glance at the time, the lawman frowned.

"You've just lost five minutes, Mr. Bluss," Ments warned him. "I'd hurry along if I was you."

"The nearest town's fifteen miles away," pleaded the tycoon. "Please, Marshal! This ain't justice! You're a man of the law. You swore an oath!"

"Tell that to my family," Ments replied before tipping his hat. "Good luck."

Bluss shuffled away to the door, past his dead pets, and opened it in the face of a torrential downpour. Unarmed and ill-equipped, he looked for his pursuers in the thick foliage, finding nothing but an innocent-looking trail.

After a moment's hesitation, Bluss clumsily ran off into the storm.

BLIND BASTARD

On a brightly-lit stage, Joshua Clements, commonly known as "Blind Bastard," performed for fifteen thousand cheering Chicago-area rock fans. The middle-aged bad boy ruled the stage with his smooth voice and brilliant guitar style. He wore a wildly patterned purple-and-black silk shirt, black jeans, gray cowboy boots, and a stylish pair of black sunglasses. Tall and lanky, he strummed his white guitar with fiery grace as he finished the night's last song.

His band, *Drunken Muse,* barely managed to keep up. Covered in sweat, the aspiring rock legend thanked the audience and wished them good night. The band bowed and started to leave, except for the keyboardist. He stepped up and helped Blind Bastard offstage, seeing as Clements really was blind.

Paparazzi, roadies, and VIP fans awaited him backstage. The keyboardist handed Blind Bastard off to Neil Gurson, one of the band's personal assistants. The chubby twenty-nine-year-old underling sweated in his tieless beige suit as he politely ushered Blind Bastard through the crowd of media and fans.

Neil explained to everyone else that they were late for yet another ritzy, post-concert bash uptown and couldn't pause for comments. Five beefy-looking, black-clad security experts escorted them to the limo. The rocker kept a grin on his face, awkwardly shook a few hands, and accepted a few kisses from a pair of gorgeous twin sisters who smelled (and felt) quite nice.

"One helluva show, boss," Neil yelled over the crowd.

Blind Bastard pulled a black rubber band from off his right wrist.

"You don't have to keep sucking up Neil," replied the rocker as he tied his ten-inch mane of black hair into a ponytail.

"I'm not," Neil admitted as they reached the limo. "You know I hate concerts. Bands normally sound their best in a studio and rarely on the first take. But you guys actually sound better live. That's hard to do."

"While I think you're absolutely right," Blind Bastard grinned with a pat on Neil's arm, "I still think you're hunting for an early raise."

Neil gave a guilty smile as their pale-faced, black-uniformed chauffer opened the door for them. Blind Bastard got in first. Neil followed. The burly chauffer shut the door, sat down in the driver's seat, and drove. Neil signaled the chauffer to raise the vehicle's black opaque partition. With a nod, the chauffer complied.

"What about the guys?" Blind Bastard asked. The band always went to these parties together. It made for a better photo op.

"They wanted to shower up," Neil lied as he nervously eyed the wet bar. "Apparently, some A-list movie divas are going to be at this event."

"Sounds like the guys I grew up with," Blind Bastard grinned as he reclined into the leather seating.

He took a quick whiff and realized that he didn't smell so great either. Not that it mattered. Where he was going, the air should smell of smoke, weed, and clashing perfumes. Still, the rock star figured he'd get himself a shower later on—with a busty groupie or two to help with the hard-to-reach places.

"Care for a drink?"

"Yeah," Blind Bastard replied. "They set us up with the usual?"

"Oh yeah," Neil replied as he quietly pulled a small vial of gray powder from inside his suit jacket.

"Then start me off with a scotch, my good man."

"Will do, boss."

Neil slipped the powder into an empty glass, dumped two ice cubes inside, and then poured the scotch. He twirled the glass around a bit and then passed it on to Blind Bastard. The rock star downed it with practiced ease.

"Another, please."

"Coming right up," Neil replied as he poured Blind Bastard another glass, minus any additional powder.

From what Neil was told, the sedative should run through Clements' system in ten seconds and render him unconscious within five more. Neil handed his boss the second helping, watched it go down, and then glanced at his watch. Sure enough, Blind Bastard started to say something, drunkenly blinked, and then passed out into Neil's lap.

The assistant checked his boss' pulse for a nervous few seconds. Then a relieved grin crossed Neil's face as he knocked three times on the partition and slid out from under the helpless rock star. The limo came to a stop. The partition slid down and the chauffer glanced over at Blind Bastard.

"Any problems?" the chauffer asked with an oddly-accented voice.

"Nope," Neil replied, fully aware that he was past the point of no-return.

The men who hired him to set up Blind Bastard approached him a month ago with two million in cash.

Once he spent a few days counting it all, Neil parked it in a hard-to-find, offshore account. In a few months, after Neil persuaded everyone that he had nothing to do with the kidnapping, he'd enjoy spending it.

"Well, I'd better play frightened and deliver the ransom note," Neil said as he eagerly hit the door lock for the rear-left door.

Nothing happened.

About to complain, he looked up into the barrel of the chauffer's suppressor-capped pistol. Neil managed a trembling whimper before two slugs went through his forehead. Gun in hand, the chauffer smoothly exited the limo and glanced around. In the cool autumn night, the driver's brown eyes turned a deep shade of yellow as they blinked. The limo was parked near a small grade school. Around them was a quiet, blue-collar neighborhood on the outer edge of the city. As arranged, no one else was around this late at night.

The chauffer pulled a white, marble-shaped communications device from his pocket and muttered something in a truly alien tongue. Seconds later, both he and the limo disappeared in a blinding flash of white light.

Several Earth hours later, Blind Bastard woke up in a Judgment Chair, minus his sunglasses. The metallic chair's thick, leathery straps tightly bound him by the limbs, waist, and neck. But the "prisoner" hadn't noticed his restraints yet. Were it not for the foggy after-effects of the sedative, the rocker would've been scared, angry, or some mixture of both. Instead, he was too busy wondering why this dream was so real.

Around him was a large, dome-shaped audience hall filled with over forty thousand sentients from hundreds of different worlds. While Blind Bastard couldn't see them, he could hear them. They chattered like a stadium full of rock fans waiting for the next show to start. A pillar of hot red light suddenly fell upon him like a July sun. Blind Bastard groaned with irritation. Grand Adjudicator Oralm, a brawny alien with a humanoid appearance, entered the room. Oralm could almost pass for human, save for the feline whiskers, thick purple skin, and a single white square of bone that jutted from his forehead like a blunted horn. His red-and-black robes denoted his supreme rank among those who judged criminals within this galaxy. Unlike the judges on Earth, his verdict was final.

"Graysal Irmund," the Grand Adjudicator began, in his native tongue, which sounded like a deep-throated clicking to Blind Bastard, "you are hereby accused of numerous crimes against the Commonwealth of Sentient Races. How do you plead?"

"Man," Blind Bastard muttered with a shake of his head as he opened his sightless blue eyes. "I passed out from two glasses of scotch?"

Oralm cocked his head to the left and then tapped his translator. The red, collar-shaped device was snugly wrapped around his thick neck.

"Graysal Irmund," Oralm asked again, his words sounding off in fluent English. "How do you plead?"

Blind Bastard tried to get up and finally realized that he was restrained.

"Whoa!" the now-angry rocker exclaimed. "Who the fuck tied me up?!"

"We did," replied the Grand Adjudicator. "You're back on Korath, where you will stand trial for genocide, high treason, piracy, and dozens of other crimes."

Blind Bastard grinned as he tested his restraints.

"What is this? C'mon guys! Isn't it a bit too late in the day for interviews or prank shows?"

Murmurs from the audience increased as they heard the conversation through their assorted translation devices.

"What is a 'prank show'?" Oralm asked, curious.

"Very funny," Blind Bastard grinned with fake mirth. "Now let me out of this dentist chair, willya'? I gotta piss."

"You've much to answer for, General."

Blind Bastard sniffed the air. Aside from his own stink, his nose took in a bunch of other scents he had never encountered before. Since that batch of his cousin's poorly-made moonshine blinded him eight years ago, he had learned to trust his sense of smell.

He wasn't at an after-concert party.

Nor was he in his hotel room.

Blind Bastard's face twisted with fear at the realization that this wasn't some kind of prank.

"Am I being kidnapped?"

"No," Oralm snarled, his patience waning.

He waved a finger in front of Blind Bastard's face and realized that accused couldn't see. The Grand Adjudicator's face twisted with embarrassed annoyance.

"Fit the General with optical implants," Oralm commanded as he turned and walked away. "We'll resume the trial tomorrow."

Blind Bastard was snatched from his chair, placed under heavy guard, and sent to a xeno-medical facility. The rocker shouted, cursed, made futile attempts at bribery . . . and then pissed himself. After that, the aliens anesthetized him and removed his eyes. In the place of his baby blues were custom-crafted implants which would allow him to see again.

When Blind Bastard opened his new silver-hued eyes and regarded his captors, he shrieked with fear and then fainted like a man.

*   *   *

"What do you mean he's not General Irmund?!" Oralm bellowed.

General Sirgith, his chief aide, was the only other sentient in the room. He wore a gray uniform with eight red stripes along the middle, to denote his rank. Huge and black-furred, the simian-faced aide folded his four arms as he paced past Oralm, equally stumped by the current situation.

"We have run every test imaginable," Sirgith explained. "We did not find any signs of cloning, surgical mimicry, or even nanoshapeshifting. The prisoner is a natural-born human."

"Did you contact our agents on Earth?" Oralm asked.

"Yes sir," Sirgith replied. "I reviewed their mission files myself. First, they received an anonymous tip that Irmund was on Earth. A team was sent to collect samples from him, samples which matched perfectly with our records. Our labs triple-checked the data, sir—"

"This is Irmund's doing!" Oralm thundered, his skin turning bright orange with rage. "Somehow, he arranged this. But why frame a blind human?"

"With respect," Sirgith advised. "I am more concerned about how he managed to fool us so thoroughly."

"Clearly, he still has agents within the Ministry of Interstellar Justice," Oralm scowled. "And I doubt he's still on Earth. With this botched arrest, he's not only made fools of us—but he's distracted us long enough to flee. But where?"

"Give me time," Sirgith vowed. "I will find out."

Oralm nodded to Sirgith, one of his most trusted officers, confident that the general would get to the bottom of this ruse. The Grand Adjudicator turned and started to leave.

"What of the human?" Sirgith asked.

Oralm paused, bothered by having to deal with the insignificant lifeform. Still, the poor fool was an innocent. He turned toward an observation portal and looked up into Korath's night sky, deep in thought.

Sirgith's personal beltcom chimed twice. Shaped like a large metal clam, it was dwarfed by the alien's lower-left hand as he picked it up and activated the device's holodisplay. A square-shaped light projection appeared from the beltcom and produced a real-time image of the caller. The general's obsidian eyes widened at the sight of a young human with a sunny tropical background behind him.

Tanned, tall, and gleeful, he looked like a younger version of Joshua Clements—only with more muscles. Sprawled out on his back, upon a white beach chair, he looked quite comfortable. The near double wore red-tinted sunglasses, a pair of yellow swimming trunks, and black flip-flops. Sounds of wild music, partying, and splashing water could be heard in the background.

"Sirgith!" Irmund greeted joyously in Ur'Pay, the standard language of the Commonwealth. "My favorite, monkey-faced official! How are you, you four-armed tree humper?!"

Oralm rushed over and glared down at the holodisplay. While the being looked human and spoke with a human voice, both aliens knew that it was Irmund.

"Oralm?!" Irmund grinned. "How's the wife and kittens?"

"I'll personally feed you to them when this over!" the Grand Adjudicator scowled.

"You need to try some yoga, Your Honour," Irmund mocked. "It's good for the soul."

"What do you want, you traitorous filth?" Sirgith sneered.

"Just three small favors and I'm out of your lives for good. I won't expose your little faux pas to the public and possibly screw up your fragile little Commonwealth."

"How dare you presume to ask me for anything!" Oralm yelled. "You're a traitor, murderer, pirate, and thief! You deserve to die for the lives you've taken –"

Irmund interrupted the judge with a loud fart. A bit embarrassed, the rogue general shrugged to someone off-screen.

"I have a permanent case of Carssian Mentalysis," Irmund said, with a "duh!" in his expression. "While your doctors say it makes my kind crazy-evil, I prefer the term . . . 'special.' I was doing great things for the Commonwealth, killing folks too inferior to belong in our civilized society. Folks far worse than me."

Irmund's mouth twisted with a sudden ire of his own.

"And after all my years of service, you didn't think twice about ordering me incinerated, you maggot motherfuckers!"

"There's no cure for Mentalysis," Oralm growled. "And you knew too many Commonwealth secrets to simply be locked away, where anyone with the means could get to you."

Irmund mockingly chuckled, in no way accepting that justification.

"I could see the 'wisdom' of your actions. You can see the madness of mine. Let's agree to disagree and get down to business."

"What do you want?" Oralm asked.

"Well, Your Honour, my first request is that you delete any and all files on yours truly: military records, psychological files, and so forth."

"Why?" Sirgith asked. "Your misdeeds are well-known."

"Let's just say I'd rather be more myth than fact," Irmund replied with an even smile. "My second favor is for you bureaucrats to leave me alone. No capture teams or open-ended bounties on my life. Though, I guess I could tolerate you watching my every move, via surveillance units. Just don't block my sun, okay?"

Oralm's clawed fists clenched.

"You're lucky we can't find you, you miserable piece of—"

"Malibu," Irmund interrupted. "I'm in Malibu. It's a quaint spot on Earth, by the sea. Even though I'm no longer aquatic, I still love playing in the water. If you want, I could give you exact coordinates. Just remember: if I disappear or die from anything but a ripe old age, your unadoring public will know about every dirty little deed we've ever done."

Oralm and Sirgith exchanged worried glances.

Prior to the Mentalysis, Irmund was in charge of many of the Ministry's black ops, second only to Sirgith himself. He was once entrusted to save the Commonwealth from threats too "unique" for the law to handle. Operations that were highly illegal. If they ever came to light, some of the Commonwealth's member worlds might secede and trigger an all-out civil war.

"What's your third demand?" Oralm tensely asked.

"Kill Joshua Clements," the rogue general demanded, his demeanor dead serious. "Make it sweet and quick, like he was . . . oh . . . 'shot while trying to escape.'"

"Why are you so eager to kill this one human?" Sirgith asked.

"I liked his music so much that I wanted to be him," the mad alien replied. "But since that kind of PR spin is impossible—even in this world—I opted to have my genes remade to match those of a theoretical love child of the great Blind Bastard."

"You want to pose as a child of his?" Oralm frowned.

"Got it in one, Your Honour," Irmund beamed. "I knew you were smarter than you looked. I'm Clements' bastard son, he never knew I existed, yadda-yadda. It's an odd retirement but a fun one, too."

Oralm and Sirgith stared at each other again.

"In exchange for these three favors, I hereby vow to never leave Earth. This place is so crazy that I feel normal here. Furthermore, I will dismantle any and all of my criminal enterprises in Commonwealth space. The interstellar crime rate in your neck of the woods should plummet overnight."

Oralm stood stock-still, immersed in the possibilities.

"Again," Irmund said with dead-serious emphasis, "you have my word."

Irmund was evil, deranged, and worthy of a painful death . . . but he always kept his word, even after the Mentalysis took his mind. While he could happily pose as the bastard son of his latest victim, and spout a string of lies about it, the rogue couldn't break a vow. That twisted sort of honesty was, ironically, his last redeeming quality.

"So, do we have an agreement?" Irmund asked as a beautiful woman in a white bikini handed him a Mojito.

Joshua Clements sat in his metal cell and enjoyed a bowl of red protein noodles. His thoughts danced around from almost being mistakenly executed, to wondering how many alien races there were, to why he never became a Trekkie as a child. But mainly, he was happy to have his sight back . . . even though his eyes were now a funny shade of silver. Once he realized that these aliens had their version of "due process," Josh knew that he'd be okay. He expected them to figure out that he wasn't some alien war criminal and then send him home.

Once he got back, the rocker planned to ditch his stupid nickname and live his life right. While he probably wouldn't go to church every Sunday, Josh would ease up on the partying . . . a bit. Although he was thirty-eight, Joshua Clemmons felt reborn. There were so many things he could do again: from hunting to surfing. While he had his music, fame, and friends, his former blindness had occasionally depressed him. But now, he felt nothing but optimism at what his future held.

The rocker made a mental note to make some hefty donations to organizations dealing with UFO sightings. And he could go back to sizing up women by the way they looked instead of how they felt and smelled: the way God meant for him to. He even began to toy with the idea of starting a family.

It felt good to be whole again.

The door to his cell slid open and in strode Sirgith. As the cell door slid closed, the rock star set his meal aside and rose to his feet. Josh regarded the four-armed alien's stern expression and realized that he wasn't bearing good news. Sirgith tapped his gray translation collar.

"I am General Sirgith, chief aide to Grand Adjudicator Oralm."

"That's nice," Josh nodded with his most bland celebrity tone. "Can I go home now?"

"No," Sirgith evenly replied. "You have been found guilty of crimes against the Commonwealth and will be executed tomorrow."

A shudder went through Josh as his pseudo-calm façade turned into a frightened anger.

"But I'm not this alien war criminal that you're looking for!"

"We know—"

"I'm human!" Josh interrupted as he began to pace around his cell. "A rock star! I've been blind for eight fucking years! Seeing as I live light years away, I've got a damned-good alibi, right?!"

"We know you're innocent," Sirgith cut in with a loud, forceful tone.

"You can't just kidnap . . . W-What?" Josh blinked, clearly confused.

The alien sized up the human's surprised reaction and calmed himself. Sirgith's anger was misplaced. The aide was shamed at what Oralm had ordered him to do. Were it not for his fierce devotion to the Commonwealth, Sirgith would've sent this human back to his inferior world and been done with him.

But this was not to be.

"The Ministry of Justice, which is responsible for maintaining law and order throughout hundreds of worlds, has just been fooled into arresting the wrong person. This trial was much-anticipated. And should our error be made public . . ."

Sirgith paused to search for the right words to make this human understand what was at stake.

"What happens?" Josh pressed.

"Such a mistake—such a failure—would severely damage the otherwise-respected reputation of the Ministry."

Josh paused to take this in for a moment. Then he paced toward the opposite wall, turned, and regarded Sirgith.

"You cut a deal with this asshole?!"

Sirgith nodded as he approached the rock star.

"Were he to release our secrets," the alien continued, "the assembled members of the Commonwealth would see the Ministry as both incompetent and corrupt. Then our civilization could fall amidst chaos and blood. Millions—perhaps billions—of innocents would die."

"But you are incompetent and corrupt!" Josh yelled with an exasperated sweeping of his arms.

"Yes," Sirgith sighed with regret. "Perhaps you are right."

Then the alien lashed out with his upper-right fist and drove it straight through Josh's surprised face. The force of the blow shattered bone and brain as Josh's body left the floor and bounced off the opposite wall. Sirgith looked down at his bloodied, four-finger hand.

"Perhaps you were right," Sirgith amended as he turned to walk away and report that General Graysal Irmund was killed during a daring escape attempt.

MUNCHIES

Donovan sat on a metal park bench, bathed in the glow of a nearby streetlight. A dark-skinned Haitian, his loose-fitting thug attire easily covered his short and skinny frame. He appeared to be in his mid-thirties, with long black dreadlocks and a well-trimmed four-inch beard.

A large white joint loosely danced in the fingers of his right hand. At his feet were the stubbed-out remnants of five others just like it. With practiced ease, Donovan struck a wooden match, lit up, and leaned back. Then he exhaled a plume of smoke, stared up at the night sky, and enjoyed his high.

Fifteen yards away, a pair of black muggers eyed Donovan from the cover of some large green bushes. Earl was in his late 20's, large and athletic. He carried a sawed-down 12-gauge pumpgun. The sleeves of his dark-blue sweat suit were rolled up to expose his large arms. Reggie was in his early 30's, shorter, very overweight, and armed with a 9mm pistol. Reggie wore dark blue jeans, a black t-shirt, and matching high tops.

The long-time friends-turned-muggers ducked back behind the bushes.

"Never saw this cat before," Reggie whispered.

"Think he's waitin' for someone?" Earl asked.

"We hit him fast enough, it won't matter."

Something about this pothead didn't look right to Earl. Nobody just sat in the park and smoked blunts outside—not in this neighborhood. It was a fast way to get jumped by crack fiends, police, or muggers (like Earl and Reggie).

Reggie checked his gun.

"Let's do this."

Earl nervously nodded and followed. They closed in stealthily enough. The smoker never sensed them coming. All they had to do was get this dude's cash and bounce before anything could go wrong. Then (maybe) he'd get home to his girl and infant son with enough loot to last until he could find some honest work.

This "snatch-and-grab" shit's gettin' old, Earl thought.

When they were close enough, Reggie signaled Earl to do his thing.

Earl put the shotgun to the back of Donovan's head, just as the Haitian took a long drag from his fiery joint. The victim tensed and then froze as Reggie moved around the bench. He shifted the pistol into his left hand and cocked the hammer. Donovan sized Reggie up for a moment. Then, the Haitian blew a casual smoke ring. As he slowly raised both hands, the "victim" seemed more amused than afraid.

"Run your loot," Reggie commanded.

Donovan stuck the joint between his teeth and carefully emptied his pockets. The haul was impressive. He had car keys with a Lexus emblem chain, a thick wad of cash, a red cell phone, and a baggie with eight rolled joints in it.

"The watch, too," Reggie ordered.

As Donovan complied, Earl grinned at the cash on the ground. The sight of Ben Franklin's face put a smile on his. Reggie looked equally elated as he tucked his gun away and pocketed Donovan's possessions. The Haitian gently backed his head against the barrel of Earl's shotgun, inhaled his joint . . . and moved.

Earl gawked as Donovan snatched the shotgun's barrel with his left hand and jerked it forward. Instinctively, Earl tried to pull back the 12-gauge—with his index finger still on the trigger. As the shotgun went off, Donovan made sure that the barrel was pointed in Reggie's direction. Reggie's corpse hit the ground, minus half its shocked face. Blood, brains, and bone fragments splattered in all directions.

With a growl, Donovan snatched the shotgun away like the larger man was a toddler. Shocked, Earl backed off as Donovan stood up and frowned down at his blood-soaked clothing. His pearly-white upper incisors grew into vampire fangs.

"Dammit mon!" Donovan hissed with a thick Haitian accent. "Didja' have to ruin my new threads?!"

The vampire dropped the shotgun and spat out his joint. Earl shrieked and ran away. Donovan casually ripped the park bench off its moorings and lobbed it after the fleeing human with both hands. The well-thrown bench clipped Earl across the back and knocked him down. Donovan picked up his dropped joint, brushed it off, and then took a deep drag. After a moment's thought, he sauntered over to the injured mugger with a hungry smile. Earl grasped his lower back as Donovan reached him.

"All this weed's makin' me hungry," Donovan muttered as he circled the injured human.

"Please don't kill me!"

"Don't have to," Donovan nodded toward Reggie's corpse. "Your friend's blood's still good for a while."

Donovan then stopped and knelt next to Earl, his deep brown eyes narrowed with hunger.

"But I could use me some munchies."

"Food?!" Earl asked.

"Yeah, mon! Why d'ya think I'm smoking all this good shit at once?! Eating real food makes me feel human again. And ganja's the only thing that makes me hungry enough to eat it."

It was the fear that kept Earl from having a "what-the-fuck" moment.

"There's a store right around the corner," he fast-talked.

"And a soul food restaurant's right next door," Donovan said as he patted Earl on the head like a cute little mutt. "But I can't walk in, all covered in blood and brains, now can I? So, you limp on down and bring me back two slabs of ribs, a six-pack of Miller, a bag of Doritos, and some Skittles. Any flavor's fine."

Earl winced as he struggled to rise.

"N-no problem."

"Better not be," Donovan muttered as he stooped and helped Earl to his feet. As he did, the vampire gave his would-be mugger a quick sniff. "I smell a woman's scent on ya' . . . and a baby's too. If you ain't back in thirty minutes, they'll be dessert. Understand?"

Earl vigorously nodded, his face twisted with layers of fear.

"Off you go."

Earl turned and limped off as fast as his battered body would let him.

"Mm-mm-mm!" Donovan smiled as he dropped the last rib bone into a styrofoam box. "That sauce is almost sweeter than blood!"

Earl's heart pounded.

It wasn't just from the mad dash for food—or the way he had to threaten a little old lady for the last pack of Skittles in the store. It was when Earl came back to find Donovan feeding on his best friend's corpse. At the sight of his munchies, the vampire punted Reggie off into the night like he was a football. Then, Donovan retracted his incisors, directed the mugger to a nearby picnic table, and ravaged the food.

"You did good, mon!" Donovan said with a grin.

Earl exhaled with relief at the thought that his family wasn't on the menu. As far as he was concerned, his life of crime was over as of thirty minutes ago.

"I'm gonna shit like a goose," Donovan said, after a hearty belch. "But it's a small price to pay, y'know?"

Donovan finished his last can of beer, tossed it into a metal garbage can, and then got up to leave. A weirdly-brilliant idea bounced into Earl's head with such force that it made him wince.

"Wait."

The vampire stopped and turned around.

"You're not the only vampire in town, are you?"

"Oh no, mon! There's quite a few of us," Donovan laughed. "Why you ask? You want to join the club?"

"Naw," Earl replied. "I was just wondering if . . . you'd wanna partner up?"

Donovan approached Earl slowly, a curious but dangerous gleam in his eye.

"Say again?"

"A sort of catering or delivery service," Earl offered. "One-part weed, one-part munchies. It might be good for vamps who want to feel human for a day. We could call it *Night Snacks* or some shit like that. Think it would fly?"

Donovan folded his arms with a thoughtful frown, scratched his bearded chin, and then regarded the mortal for a long moment. Then a sly smile crept over his blood-stained face.

"Tell me more," replied the vampire.

DEMON EYES

Roy Quettle burst into Dr. Dael's reception area. The lanky nineteen-year-old wore black jeans, a yellow button-down shirt, a pair of black sunglasses, and a noticeable amount of sweaty panic. He ignored the three seated patients and headed straight for the receptionist's desk. There sat Gladys, Dr. Dael's long-time receptionist. Well into her 50's, the pudgy-faced woman calmly eyed the panicked Roy with her fake office smile.

"Hello, Roy. What can I—?"

"Dr. Dael!" Roy frantically asked. "Where's Doc Dael?!"

"He's with a patient," Gladys replied with growing concern. "What's wrong, Roy?"

"I need him right now!" Roy said as he turned toward Dr. Dael's office. "It's an emergency!"

"If you'll just wait a—" Gladys began before Roy turned and ran across the reception area.

"Roy!" Gladys called after him. "Roy! He's with a patient!"

Roy opened the door to the examination room to find it darkened. Dr. Michael Dael looked up from the eye test he was administering to an elderly gentleman. The short, brown-bearded optometrist was in his mid-40's. His normally kind face abruptly frowned at the intrusion as Roy flipped on the lights.

"I'm sorry to barge in here, doc. But I need your help!"

Gladys reached the door a few seconds later, breathing hard.

"What's wrong, Roy?" Dr. Dael asked.

Roy took off the sunglasses.

Both of his eyes were deep crimson. No pupils or irises—just blood-hued orbs. Dr. Dael's patiently gasped at the sight and crossed himself.

After apologetically rescheduling the elderly patient's checkup, Dr. Dael re-entered his office to find Roy trembling in the examination chair. The optometrist closed the door and folded his arms. He had known Roy since kindergarten. He was nearsighted and wore regular contacts for about five years now. There wasn't anything this exotic in Roy's file (or he'd have remembered it). Simply put, his blood red eyes made no sense.

"Roy, I still think I should drive you to the hospital."

"No," Roy shook his head. "No one else can know about this."

"But there's only so much I can do," Dr. Dael said. "And your health might be at risk."

"I ain't too worried about my health right now, doc," Roy pleaded as he pointed at his eyes. "Please take them out!"

"Take what out?"

"The contacts, doc!" Roy yelled. "The contacts!"

"Contacts?" Dr. Dael cocked his head. "The ones I prescribed for you?"

"No!" Roy groaned. "I ordered some *Demon Eye* contacts off the 'Net, for Halloween. They're supposed to look like this!"

Dr. Dael rolled his eyes and sighed with a measure of relief. *So they're supposed to look that way,* he thought. *I am truly getting old.*

Why folks ordered contact lenses from these fly-by-night internet companies amazed Dr. Dael. The damned things must've had a flaw in them.

"They came in this morning and I tried 'em on," Roy whined. "I can see just fine. But they won't come out!"

Dr. Dael sighed as he reached into his shirt pocket, pulled out a penlight, and flipped it on.

"Stare straight ahead."

Roy nodded, took a deep breath, and complied. The optometrist looked in closely. Roy's eyeballs seemed to constantly ripple, like a windy pond. Mystified, Dr. Dael almost wanted to reach out and touch one.

"Have you experienced any dizziness or pain?"

"No," Roy shrugged. "Except . . ."

"What?"

Roy held up his right hand. Dr. Dael closely regarded it. Aside from the fact that his fingernails needed a bit of trimming, it looked normal enough. Then, with his left hand, Roy unbuttoned his shirt. Underneath, he wore a white t-shirt with a small golden crucifix on top of it.

"I was prayin' every prayer I knew when I was drivin' up here. I even held my cross."

Roy wrapped his right hand around the crucifix. Dr. Dael slowly backed away as white smoke rose from his patient's trembling, clenched fist. As the seconds passed, the room grew noticeably hotter and the stink of burning flesh filled the air. Unable to bear the pain any longer, Roy pulled his hand away.

"Look at my hand!"

The optometrist looked down and watched Roy's fingernails turn into black talons. A cross-shaped burn pattern, seared into his palm, quickly healed itself before their eyes! Roy sobbed and black tears ran down his cheeks. A pale Dr. Dael backed up and fumbled for the door handle.

"Doc, what's wrong with me?!" Roy sobbed.

Dr. Dael turned and ran out of the room. He grabbed Gladys by the hand and dragged her toward the front door, yelling at his waiting patients to run for their lives. Still in the chair, Roy simply sat there and cried.

"*Kill him*," purred a dark voice in Roy's mind. "*Kill them all. Feast upon their souls and grow stronger.*"

Roy slapped his black-taloned hands against his ears, drawing blackened blood. He rocked back-and-forth.

"Who are you?!" Roy yelled out as his wounds healed. "The Devil?!"

Roy heard laughter in his head.

"No, Roy. I designed those contacts. Just think of me as an eccentric old businessman who dabbles in the occult."

"I want 'em out!" Roy yelled.

"I imagine you do," the voice replied. *"But I need you, Roy. Body and soul, I need you."*

Roy looked around aimlessly as he spoke. He could not shake the feeling that he was being watched.

"Why?! I'm nobody! I work in a goddamned *Home Depot!* You've got the wrong guy!"

"You sell yourself short, Roy. Your soul's strong: so strong that you haven't succumbed to my lenses . . . not yet anyway."

"Waitaminute!" Roy shook his head. "This isn't possible! *Demon Eye* contacts can't turn wearers into real demons!"

"Really?" chuckled the mysterious speaker. *"Seeing as you have a sudden allergy to crosses, I beg to differ. Now, I know this is discomforting. But you're a killer now. Once you get out there and slaughter a few people, you'll be fine."*

"I ain't a killer!" Roy defiantly yelled.

"I can feel your heart beating, Roy. You should be feeling that urge to kill—"

"I'm not a killer!"

"You are," countered the voice. *"You've stepped on bugs, gutted fish, and hunted deer with your old man. People are lesser animals, too. Just step up and squash one, Roy. You'll like it."*

"No!" Roy shouted as he glared at his taloned fingers and desperately wanted them to turn back to normal. To his surprise, they did. Sweat ran into Roy's eyes as he smiled with renewed hope.

"See?!" Roy yelled. "I'm not a demon!"

"Oh really?"

Roy abruptly felt a stabbing pain just above his ass and jumped out of the chair. With a shriek, he turned to see a black, barbed tail punch through his jeans and writhe about.

"You're turning, Roy. Minute-by-minute, your filthy human soul is burning away, like wood in a fire. Soon, you'll be pure. Soon, you'll be mine."

Roy watched his torso, arms, and legs become more muscular to the point where his clothes' seams ripped. The bones in his ankles grew and shifted, shooting currents of unspeakable pain throughout his entire body. Roy fell back into the chair. Quickly, he kicked off his gym shoes, watched his feet burst from his white socks, and whimpered with fright as they turned into black, cloven hooves.

Catching his reflection in a mounted mirror, Roy saw his skin turn a deep crimson. Then a searing pain gripped his skull. Roy stifled a scream as he turned back toward the mirror just in time to watch smooth black horns protrude from his hairline and gently curve forward. His teeth were the same shape—but now pitch-black in hue. His now-demonic face was downright grotesque. As his clothes ripped, the crucifix touched his chest. The holy symbol barely felt warm against his hardened skin.

"Please! Just kill me!" Roy pleaded, his voice suddenly deeper and full of despair.

"Why?" asked the voice. *"You're going to serve me. And, when there are enough of you running around, so will the rest of the world."*

"There are more like me?" Roy asked with revulsion.

"You didn't think you were the only one, did you? My Chinese facility has three whole shifts cranking out Demon Eye lenses. I've got marketing companies, on six continents, pushing them. There'll be about eight

hundred thousand of you running amok by Devil's Night—all attuned to my voice."

Roy breathed heavily as he looked down at the cross on his chest. A dangerous idea slipped into his mind.

"So we're linked together, you and I?"

"That's right," his impending master replied. *"I see what you see, hear what you hear, and smell what you smell. Your world is my playground!"*

Roy grinned as he ripped the cross from its chain, popped it into his mouth, and swallowed hard. The cross descended into his torso like a lump of burning coal. Roy's pain-wracked body convulsed so hard that he fell out of the chair and onto the floor. A fiery white light erupted from inside his fanged mouth.

Across the binding link, Roy heard an old man's short, undistorted wail of pure agony. The demon closed his eyes and was able to see through those of his would-be master. The occultist was in a small, cluttered room filled with shelves of books and bottled ingredients. At the center of it was a blood-soaked altar.

If the bastard really was an occultist, Roy figured that this place was probably his workshop. The old man looked down at his gray-haired chest. That allowed Roy to see a fiery-white light burn through his sternum, melting out through a fancy white shirt and gray vest.

Clearly dying, the occultist helplessly gazed into a mirror. As he did, Roy looked his tormentor in the eye—sort of. Somewhere in his early 70's, his chubby face was reddened with hellish agony and lined by a neatly-trimmed beard. Roy grinned as steam rose from the cruciform wound. Burnt flesh and hair stung Roy's nostrils as the occultist then died.

Once he did, the altar cracked down the middle severing the link. Roy's consciousness returned to Dr. Dael's office. The cross itself melted into meaningless, misshapen slag. To Roy's amazement, he was still alive, with his free will intact. Better still, the spasms stopped and the pain lessened.

Roy heard approaching footsteps.

Officers Carter and Quinn rushed into the examination room to find Roy lying "unconscious" on the floor—in human form. Guns drawn, they entered and gave the room a quick once-over. Quinn knelt over Roy and checked his pulse.

"He's alive," Quinn said.

"I'll check the other rooms," Carter replied as she cautiously headed off.

Roy stirred and opened his eyes. Quinn regarded the youth with a mixture of annoyance and relief. Dr. Dael had flagged them down on the street, screaming something about a "red-eyed monster" in his office.

The kid was probably high on something, which would—sort of—explain the ripped clothes, bare feet, and racing pulse. Quinn was cautious but felt confident that he could restrain Roy if necessary. After all, the patrolman was a 6'2, 230-pound ex-college wrestler and this kid was 170 pounds soaking wet.

Odds were that he'd just "love" to compare Dael's official statement to the kid's.

"You okay, son?" Quinn asked.

As the question left his lips, he sniffed and frowned. It smelled like something foul had been burnt in here. Roy looked up at Quinn with his brown eyes and gave the cop a hungry smile.

"Never better, officer," Roy replied. "Just a bit of eye strain."

WHIMSY

Under the heat of a glaring sun, Pierre Maffont grinned with relief at the sight of the small town ahead. The Frenchman was in his late twenties, with a fair amount of blonde stubble on his handsome face. He wore dust-hued clothing consistent with those of a Wild West drifter, down to the cowboy hat and gun belt with a loaded Colt Peacemaker.

He'd been riding through scorching desert terrain for the last three days and wanted nothing more than a cold bath and a colder drink. His white-and-brown speckled mustang stubbornly trotted onward, as if the beast knew that a trough full of water was nearby.

After another half-hour's ride, he reached a sign that welcomed him to the town of Whimsy. Pierre took in the bustle of local townsfolk as other riders passed him on horseback and on assorted horse-drawn wagons. Then he headed for the first saloon he could find. There, he tethered the mustang, which eagerly sipped from the wooden trough under the hitching post. Pierre slapped his black saddlebag over his right shoulder and entered the saloon.

A vacant piano sat at the rear wall. Six older men played poker around a corner table. They glanced his way for a moment and then returned to their game. A plain-faced woman tended bar. She wore a white apron over her sky-blue dress with her black hair tied up in a bun. In her early forties, she had a tall frame that didn't offend the eye. Pierre took a seat at the bar and removed his hat.

"What can I get you?" the woman asked with a pleasant smile.

"A beer and a shot of whiskey please," he answered with a thick French accent.

The bartender gave him a second look as she reached for an empty mug.

"You from Louisiana?"

"No," Pierre grinned as she filled his glass with beer. "France."

"Really?" she asked before sliding his cold beer across the bar.

Too thirsty to reply, he caught the mug in hand and drained a fifth of it on the spot.

"Pierre Maffont," he said, after pulling his lips away from the mug.

"Evelyn Conroy," the bartender replied with a polite smile.

Pierre sipped from his glass.

"France must be quite a bit different than Texas," Evelyn mused as she reached for a shot glass and an unmarked bottle of whiskey.

"You could say that," Pierre nodded with a shy smile. "It's so much hotter here."

"You'll get used to it," the bartender grinned as she poured his whiskey and walked it over.

"Thank you," Pierre smiled as he tossed some coins on the bar and downed the shot.

"Passing through or planning to stay a while?" Evelyn asked as she pocketed the coins.

Pierre took another swallow from his beer mug.

"That depends," Pierre cryptically sighed as he pulled a brown pouch of tobacco and some white paper from his saddlebag. With dexterous efficiency, he began to roll himself a cigarette.

"On what?" Evelyn pressed.

"I'm looking for someone. And I think he lives here."

"Well," Evelyn offered, "I've resided here for fifteen years. If this 'someone' is living in Whimsy, I'll know him."

"His name's Theodore Rowfeld," Pierre said.

Evelyn winced at the mention of the name. The men at the poker table also glanced up at the mention of Rowfeld.

"He left town six weeks back," Evelyn explained. "Would you happen to know where he was headed?"

"No," she replied after a few seconds of thought. "He just up and left one day. It took us a few days to notice that he was gone."

Pierre's face fell as he stuck the finished cigarette into his mouth, struck a match, and raised it to his cigarette.

"I'm sorry to hear that," he said. "Then I guess I'm just passing through then."

"Was he a friend of yours?"

"No," Pierre replied. "I was hoping to learn from him."

"Learn what?" Evelyn asked with a frown. "He used to be our town drunk. That's all he knew how to do."

"Once upon a time, he was the greatest artist in the world," Pierre said. "While he never publicly presented his works, he was revered in certain circles."

Two of the old card players chuckled at the idea. Even Evelyn regarded Pierre with a fair amount of skepticism.

"And you're an artist, too?"

"Yes," Pierre nodded as he reached into his saddlebag and pulled out a book of landscape sketches.

Evelyn wiped her hands on her apron and then opened them. Pierre gripped his cigarette with his left hand and finished his beer with his right. As he did,

Evelyn looked through his sketches with an admiring eye.

"You're pretty darned good, Pierre!"

"Thank you," grinned the artist as he took a drag of his cigarette. "But I'm not half as good as Rowfeld."

"Aren't there other art teachers?" Evelyn asked as she returned his sketchbook. "Folks who aren't town drunks?"

"Of course," Pierre nodded as he exhaled a plume of smoke. "But none of them knew what he knows. Rowfeld could paint a landscape so real that it became its own, separate world."

"He must've been good!" Evelyn laughed. "Of course, I remember his hands being pretty shaky when he didn't have a bottle in them."

"Is that so?" Pierre frowned.

"Afraid so. It's a shame you came all this way," Evelyn said. "We've got a room upstairs to rent—if you're interested."

"That would be nice," Pierre replied with a polite smile.

After Evelyn showed Pierre his room and handed him the key, he locked up the saddlebag. Then, he left his horse at the town stable and took a stroll. Whimsy was quite the pleasant little place. It wasn't just the friendly people or the odd fact that the town wasn't as scorching hot as the surrounding desert. It was the fact that he found Whimsy to be calm and soothing—an effect that seemed to be clear on the faces of everyone around him.

Just before sunset, Pierre headed back to the saloon with a bag of apples and some beef jerky from the general store.

"Evenin'," a voice called out from behind.

Pierre turned around to see the town sheriff and two of his deputies slowly heading his way with a wary look about them. The graying-haired, stocky sheriff tilted his gray cowboy hat upwards.

"You must be the Frenchman everyone's been talking about," smiled the sheriff as he held out a hand. "Emmitt Durke. And these two fine gentlemen are my deputies."

"Pierre Maffont," the artist replied as he shook the sheriff's hand. "Is there a problem?"

"You could say that, Pierre."

The two deputies looked on with quiet menace.

"See," Durke smiled, "we know why you're really here. You wanted to learn how to paint a mystical landscape."

"'A mystical landscape?'" Pierre laughed, sincerely confused. "No, I merely wanted to learn art from a true master."

"Heh!" scoffed the lawman. "What year is this, son?"

"1881," Pierre replied with a quizzical frown.

"No, it's not," Durke said. "It's 1954. Don't you remember?"

"Remember what?"

"Never mind, son," Durke muttered as he whipped out his gun.

Pierre dropped his bag and held up his hands.

"Wait! I can leave—"

Durke shot the Frenchman square in the chest. Pierre fell backward and landed on the wooden boardwalk. He stared up at the twilight sky as a woman screamed in the background. Evelyn ran up to Pierre and knelt beside him. Durke holstered his gun and regarded the dying young artist with a hint of guilt as he turned and led his deputies away. A crowd of onlookers formed around him.

"You never belonged here, Pierre," Evelyn said as she gently placed his head upon her knees.

Pierre tried to speak but all that came out of his mouth was blood. Evelyn reached into her apron's inner pocket and pulled out a small, leather-bound book. His vision began to blur as she gently placed the book in his hands.

"Rowfeld wanted me to pass this on to any real artists who came looking for him," she explained with a sad smile. "He said something about it being enough for you to continue. I hope you find him."

Evelyn then leaned over and kissed Pierre on the forehead as he died in her arms.

Pierre gasped as he awoke on the gallery floor.

A dozen or so people stood around him, all dressed in early-1950's attire. The second-year art student was relieved to find himself back in a small gallery in Soho—alive and unharmed. He looked down at his rumpled gray suit and thought he had just fainted. But then he noticed the leather-bound book in his hands and the aftertaste of a Whimsy apple in his mouth.

That made him smile.

"I'm all right," Pierre announced as he rose to his feet. "I just had a little too much to drink. Sorry."

There were murmurs as he got up and brushed himself off.

The art student was quickly forgotten as everyone else returned to their various activities. Pierre turned to face the landscape painting behind him. It was titled, *A Day In Whimsy*. The painting was done by Theodore Rowfeld, an up-and-coming artist who mysteriously disappeared a few weeks ago. Pierre had been invited to the show by some classmates and came across Rowfeld's works, which he found to be so realistic that they were better than full-color photos.

He asked some of the other presenting artists about Rowfeld but didn't learn much. He felt compelled to learn how Rowfeld made his paintings so lifelike. That's why Pierre wanted (no, needed) to find Rowfeld. The last thing he could remember was touching this painting (which was strictly taboo). But he couldn't help himself. It was so mesmerizing. After that, everything else seemed like a weird dream.

But it was very real—in a way. That, within this mass of canvas and paint, was a living and breathing town called Whimsy. Pierre also realized that this wasn't the only landscape painting that Rowfeld had done. There were six more—all landscapes of different places at different points in history. Rowfeld might be in one of them, waiting to teach someone his secret style.

As he clutched the book to his chest, Pierre somehow knew that Rowfeld was waiting for him.

DISPOSABLE ASSETS

Jey Ner' Wenin lay on his prison bed and eyed the darkened ceiling of his single-bed cell with a quiet, unending frustration. In his late four hundred and sixties, the alien's consciousness now resided within a balding, brutish human named Henry Glosska. Covered with anti-Semitic tattoos and a pale mix of flab and muscle, Jey wondered what dung-eating bureaucrat decided to stick him inside of this foul-breathed excuse for a sentient.

At least the last human he inhabited didn't have genital warts! Jey scowled as he scratched his itchy groin. The convict's thoughts went back to his original body. It had been ceremonially cremated after his conviction for involuntary genocide. Jey missed his body's purple skin, yellow fur, and three jet-black eyes. But most of all, he missed his former physical prowess. Born on the heavy-gee world of Minkanth, Jey's race was far superior to humanity.

In older, less-enlightened times, his people would have slaughtered the human population and turned the Earth into a vacation spot. But since they joined the Starfarer's League (with its many rules and by-laws), Jey's people became civilized. Instead of taking over known space, the Minkanthu pursued intergalactic commerce and enacted stiff laws against killing inferior species for profit.

He had endured this undignified situation for one hundred and fifty-one years. By his calculations, Jey was roughly a tenth of the way through his five consecutive life sentences for infecting the Miquan homeworld with a heart-eating virus.

It wasn't out of any particular malice.

He was merely selling some high-end viral ordinance and one of the canisters had a faulty seal. Luckily, Jey brought along enough antidote shots for everyone present or they would've died most horribly that night. Ironically, his client didn't mind, seeing as Jey replaced the lost canister for free. And most sentients felt that the universe was better off without the Miquan, who were such obnoxious bastards anyway.

If that same client hadn't given him up to the authorities a year or so later, Jey might still be the spacefaring merchant of death his dear motherbot raised him to be. The only bright side to that ill-fated contract was that the authorities never found the daza crystals he had been paid for the shipment. Should Jey ever escape from this backwater world, he'd be one rich sentient. Escape, however, seemed to be quite impossible. For one thing, he was stuck in a supermax prison called Pelican Bay. Just based on his superior intellect alone, Jey managed to come up with eight different escape scenarios and kept them on standby. But the same "minor" problem still haunted him since the first days of his imprisonment.

An unmanned Monitor ship orbited the Earth. Invisible to both the naked eye and human technology, it kept tabs on the tens of thousands of alien convicts locked away on the planet's surface. Whenever a host body died, the prisoner's mind was automatically uploaded into the Monitor's central archive. It sent an authorization request to one of the penal stations on the other side of the universe, received parameters on a new host, and then downloaded the alien's consciousness into a new human.

Such a collision of psyches—the human's and the alien's—was quite traumatic. The human's mind instantly died as the alien's took over. Luckily, most of the human's memories were accessible by the new "tenant." From that moment on, the alien was imprisoned in that host until he/she/it died again. Naturally, alien convicts were carefully kept away from each other to reduce the odds of escape—not that anyone in the know would truly try.

In the event of an escape attempt, the Monitor would simply pluck the escapee's mind out of the host's body. Once the foolish mind was back in the Monitor's prison archive, the ship's artificial intelligence would initiate its feared "Sanction Protocol." An ex-con once told Jey that it was akin to being chopped into pieces while being burned alive. The side effect was nothing shy of a lobotomy. Then, the ruined mind would be dumped into the bodies of mentally handicapped inmates until his/her/its sentence was satisfied.

The only way to get around a Monitor would be with outside assistance.

Jey couldn't envision where he'd find the parts to make an interstellar com system, how to power it, or even who to call. Most of his contacts were long dead or too smart to risk their lives on his behalf. A few were serving multi-life terms on other primitive worlds. Plus, the Monitor would detect and intercept any such communiqué, trace it back to Jey, and then fry his mind.

There was also the matter of transport.

Before his incarceration, a starship was the only feasible escape option. That ship would have to be able to either sneak or fight its way past a Monitor—which got regular upgrades in both weapons and sensor tech. After a century-and-a-half on Earth, perhaps other options were available. But since he was cut off from other alien convicts, Jey couldn't assess them.

The convict felt a headache coming on and rolled over onto his side. He knew that there had to be a way out. If he waited long enough and pushed his mind hard enough, a way would reveal—

An abrupt, painful eternity later, Jey's mind regained "consciousness" inside of the Monitor's central archive. Within it, there was nothing to sense. Just the eerie emptiness resulting from having one's mind turned into a "file" and then uploaded into a truly complex computer.

"Convict Jey Ner 'Wenin," a mechanized male voice spoke to him in his native tongue. It had been so long since he had heard fluent Minkanthri that the disembodied convict would've smiled . . . had he a face to smile with.

"Present," he neutrally replied. "Did I die?"

"Negative," the Monitor's AI replied. "Please stand by for an incoming transmission from Delbroth."

Jey was intrigued.

Delbroth was the homeworld for the League—the overall government to which most advanced worlds belonged. Artificially forged inside of a dying sun, Delbroth housed the leadership of the League, planetary envoys, and departmental branches. In short, it was the nexus of *real* civilization.

Jey hated them.

"This is Director Chas Li 'Kuth of the League's Intelligence Branch," a female voice announced in Matherian, one of the more commonly spoken trade languages.

"Pleased to speak to someone who's not an AI or a human, ma'am," Jey replied as pleasantly as possible.

He knew that a deal of some kind would be offered. Whatever it was, he'd take it. Anything to be free. Anything to be away from that dung sphere called Earth.

"I've been authorized to grant you a conditional pardon. Interested?"

"Absolutely," Jey eagerly replied. "What are the terms?"

"Upon your acceptance, you'll become a Rank 2 operative of the Intelligence Branch. Your Monitor will psi-train you in black ops and then send you back to Earth."

Jey mentally frowned.

"The mission?"

"We've received intelligence reports that the Vudrakken have a presence on Earth," Li 'Kuth explained. "We need to locate them, assess their numbers, and ascertain their intentions. Then, you'll exterminate them all."

Jey almost asked to go back to jail.

The only race his people feared was the Vudrakken. Shapeshifting xenocannibals, they loved to feed upon weaker worlds . . . the larger the better. Earth would look like a five-course meal. By the time Jey was imprisoned, the Vudrakken had already wiped out dozens of races.

The League barely managed to defeat them after a vicious nineteen-Earth-year war. But rather than make peace treaties, the League had the good sense to drop planet killers on their homeworld and each of their colonies. The survivors scattered and fled League space. To this day, even having a bit of Vudrakken DNA was an offense punishable by death.

Now, they were back.

Within a year or two, the Vudrakken could easily conquer Earth and terraform the other planets in its solar system. Within a decade, they could have an army of billions with suitable fleets to ferry them off to new interstellar conquests.

No wonder the League was concerned.

"I'll need a suitable body, gear, and some backup," Jey said.

"The Monitor will clone you an enhanced human body for this mission. It'll almost be as strong as your original one and heal four times faster. Equipment will be provided before you're sent to the surface. You'll have three other convicts at your disposal, all trained at Rank 1."

His Rank 2 psi-training would be superior to theirs. Jey paused to digest that factor.

"You want me to lead this mission?"

"Correct," Li 'Kuth replied. "All of you are multi-lifers with an adequate understanding of this planet and its people. *You're ideal for this operation. Of the team, you have the most experience.*"

"Let me guess—you don't want to waste any of your own operatives?"

There was a brief pause. Jey wondered if he had gone too far.

"We've sent in two teams of our best infiltrators and lost contact with both," she confessed. "As far as we know, they're all dead—or worse."

"And since they're on to you, they probably have connections within the Intelligence Branch," Jey guessed.

"That's why this offer's coming straight from my desk to your Monitor ship. No one else knows about it. In theory, you'll have the element of surprise. And yes, you're all sufficient candidates because you're each disposable and deniable. Most importantly, you're all seasoned criminals, which makes you better suited to match wits with the Vudrakken."

Jey didn't agree with that last part. But he wasn't dumb enough to argue.

"What's our time frame?" Jey asked.

"Seven Earth days," Li 'Kuth replied. "I'll make contact with you every twelve hours. If you should fail to eliminate the threat by that time, I'll have to enact my contingency plan."

"Which is?"

"The Monitor will fly into Earth's orbit and drop its payload of six planet killers."

"You've loaded a prison ship with six planet killers?!" Jey balked.

"Yes," Li 'Kuth replied. "Aside from the pardon, it's in your best interest to succeed. Otherwise, the Earth will be atomized . . . with you on it."

THE VESSEL

Killing a pack of werewolves was hazardous work. Killing a pack of genetically-enhanced werewolves was beyond suicidal.

Gieter and I were tasked with "putting down" the Blood Furs, a pack of racist lycanthropes who were targeting minorities up and down the West Coast. Via a mixture of bribery and convincing threats, the FBI's managed to keep their twenty-nine-victim murder spree off the media's radar—for now. One of their special ops teams was sent to deal with the Blood Furs and never came back.

That's when Gieter and I were called in.

Our mission was a two-parter. First, we had to figure out who gave the furballs their genetic upgrades. The second part was to make everyone involved die screaming.

As for that missing FBI spec ops team, their mutilated remains were found in the Oregon backwoods. All five agents were experienced in hunting occult threats and were armed with enough silver ammo to trade on the Stock Exchange. They caught up to the Blood Furs in a wooded clearing during a full moon. Then they ambushed the furballs right as they were changing.

The agents' timing and technique were flawless. The only problem was that the damned silver bullets didn't kill beast one. While werewolves were strongest under the light of a full moon, they were also hyper-vulnerable to silver.

Instead, the spec ops team was slaughtered and eaten like two-legged rabbits. The only bright spot was that the team packed hidden cameras in their helmets, guns, and body armor. This allowed Agent Heath

Minser, oversight specialist, to sit in a nearby RV and coordinate their activities from miles away. As the slaughter continued, Minser frantically sent out an S.O.S. Over the screams of his fellow agents and friends, Minser managed to keep his cool and pass along real-time intel. Thanks to him, we weren't going in blind.

Too bad he didn't make it back.

While the Blood Furs hadn't spotted him during the night, Minser got himself killed in the impressive/reckless pursuit of payback. In direct defiance of Bureau orders, the crazy-calm bastard hacked into NSA satellites and set them to automatically track Blood Fur movements. Then he armed himself with weapons, a few hidden cameras, and a bomb vest filled with silver ball bearings. Minser figured that they'd be helpless under the light of a morning sun. Silver-proof or not, he planned on thinning the herd.

We actually watched the sat footage of Agent Minser's last stand. He caught all nine of the fuckers skinny-dipping in the middle of a shallow stream, washing off dried blood with bars of soap. Werewolves could only change during a full moon, so the lore went. They should've been easy pickings.

That wasn't quite the case.

At least they were vulnerable to silver (in the daytime, anyway). Minser picked off two of them with an Uzi before they knew what hit them. He saw the rest start to transform but didn't waste time wondering how. With his right hand, he took that submachine gun and dropped three more beasts with short, well-aimed bursts. His left hand hovered near the push-button detonator on his bomb vest.

Then one of the furballs teleported to his rear and decapitated Minser before he could set off the explosives. The surviving four Blood Furs ripped

Minser apart and fed on his remains like the animals they were. Once they changed back to normal and resumed their bath, they buried their dead and moved on.

We tracked them all the way to Salem, Oregon. Then they ditched our surveillance.

By then, the FBI reached the scene, dug up the dead Blood Furs and ran forensics. Based on the combat footage, the lab folks' original theory was that these werewolves were genetic augments. Only, their tests came back negative for any signs of mundane gene tweaks of any kind. That's when the bureau called in forensic alchemists and discovered signs of mystical augmentations.

Each lycanthrope had been given one or two additional powers: none of which were the same. The technique was unknown. While there were trace amounts of various mystical ingredients, the alchemists couldn't identify them. Totally geeked out by the discovery, the alchemists admitted that they had no idea how it was done. They guessed that whoever (or whatever) did it used cloaking magicks of some kind.

At this point, they called in the Secret Service.

We comfortably shared mystical jurisdictions with the FBI, CIA, WITSEC, and INS. We handled the worst of all mystical threats. Seeing as the President of the United States was the most popular mystical target in the world, we had to be the best. When the FBI came to us for help, we happily stepped in.

As for our rules of engagement, Gieter and I were given carte blanche to settle this matter.

"Hi," I grinned as Daryl Jaughter writhed in straight-up agony at my feet.

The hairy glyph maker had a medium build, with a dark complexion and bulging beer gut. The forty-one-year-old didn't look cute in the tight black spandex shorts or the gray *Golds Gym* t-shirt he wore. While his body hair was black, Jaughter opted to dye his thinning hair blonde (God ask me why).

Gieter lowered her silencer-capped Glock .40 pistol and admired the wound she had just placed in Jaughter's right kneecap. Tall, thin, and brunette, Amelia Gieter was the scariest woman I knew. It wasn't because she had more kills than me. Or that she was a classically-trained necromancer. It was her face that did me in.

She looked to be in her early forties, with the usual wrinkles and what-not. But if her files read true, Gieter was really thirty-one. Of course, this type of work can make one age quickly. Still, whatever her age, that attractive face was always in something of a scowl. An untrained observer would simply think she had her "game face" on.

The truth was that she had only one emotion: inconsolable rage. Looking into her icy blues was akin to staring Death in the face. Every time we made eye contact, that's what I saw. Everyone got the same expression: whether it was one of her many enemies or one of her few friends. While Gieter never spoke of her past, it was a safe bet that something horrible had happened to make her this way. Whatever it was, it left her with a permanent case of "the pent-ups," which she constantly fought to control.

The study of magic taught Gieter discipline—which she used to keep her killing urges in check. It also helped her to become one of the best agents I've ever seen. I was tempted to ask why, of all the different schools of magic, she chose necromancy. But anytime I started to ask, it was as if those eyes of hers told me to mind my own damned business.

"You bitch!" Jaughter shrieked in terrified rage, as he clamped both hands over the wound. The coastal wind caught Gieter's black pantsuit and white blouse, which made her look a bit more sinister. She glanced over at me and casually aimed for his groin. "Thanks for letting me play good cop," she purred.

"My pleasure," I replied as I drew my own silencer-capped Glock, knelt down, and gently pressed the weapon against Jaughter's skull. Remarkably, I had captured his undivided attention.

"P-Please don't kill me!" he begged.

"Mr. Jaughter," I grinned, "killing you would an absolute fucking pleasure. See, my partner and I have been tracking a pack of very naughty white supremacists for about a week now."

Jaughter, who was going pale from the blood loss, now looked very queasy. If he puked on my new loafers, I'd have to shoot off some of his fingers in retaliation.

"You're feds?!"

"Of course not," I lied.

We only wore our badges at the office and on the rare instance where we weren't doing mystical black ops. It kept the Secret Service out of the papers and forced us to be more discreet in the field.

"We represent a fella with very deep pockets," I continued to fib, "whose only daughter was killed by your fleabag clients during their last full-moon rampage."

"What do you want?!" he quivered.

"I want the vessel you set up for them and the entry phrase to get in."

The glyph maker looked up at me with even greater shock. He must've figured that there was no way on God's earth that I should know about his little masterpiece. But that's the nice thing about working with a necromancer. Whenever Gieter killed someone, she absorbed their memories. We've been on this investigation for six days. During that time, we've killed eleven people tied to this particular case (without making a single arrest).

One of them, named Jeffrey Moore, was the only one who knew most of the pieces to this puzzle. The smelly prick ran an out-of-the-way motel that doubled as a safe house for the Blood Furs. We went there strictly as a procedural thing. But after we asked him a few harmless questions, he pulled a .380 and shot us both.

We let him gawk for a few seconds, just long enough to wonder why Gieter was bleeding dust and why I wasn't bleeding at all. Then we drew our guns and killed him *Pulp Fiction* style. My partner tapped into his memories and smiled.

She was able to confirm the existence of white supremacists who hooked up with like-minded werewolves and a few rogue mystics. Their plan was to form an army of lycanthropic killers with a reduced vulnerability to silver and super powers straight out of a comic book.

When their numbers were sufficient, they planned on covertly taking over the country. Some of them would assume positions of power. Others would kill anyone who got in the way. Given enough time, they might've pulled it off . . . if the Blood Furs hadn't jumped the gun and gone on an unauthorized killing spree.

The sad thing was that some of them were still human. Trusted minions, like Moore, functioned as couriers and ran safe houses for their lycanthropic counterparts. Since they weren't affected by full moons, they didn't have to worry about "wolfing out" and killing people. After enough years of loyal service, these minions would be given a promotion, via lycanthropic bite. Seeing as the motel was one of their safe houses, he knew enough about where their money came from to give Gieter a name: an oracle named Bobby Kibber.

Kibber could see one week into the future. Instead of using this power to save lives or do something noble, he opted to play the stock market as a licensed broker. While I can respect the need for greed, he only brokered for scum with deep pockets. Kibber liked the connections and intangible perks of helping maniacs triple their investments on a quarterly basis.

So, when the oracle/investor saw us coming, he did the sensible thing: he blew his brains out. We found his corpse the next day. In his suicide note, Kibber gloated that we'd fail and that America would be made pure again. He ended by claiming my pet bitch (Gieter) couldn't get him now. Hmmm. Guess he could only see the one future, where Gieter probably gunned him down and read his mind.

Well, Gieter ripped his screaming soul right out of Hell, threw it into his rotting corpse, and then read his memories—just out of spite. When she was through, the necromancer returned Kibber to his infernal reward and gave me the rest of their messed-up scheme. The supremacists hired a glyph maker to create a pocket dimension for them.

While Kibber didn't know Jaughter's name, one of Gieter's other kills surely did. Any regular glyph maker could scribble some mystical gibberish (also called a "glyph") on a regular object (called a "vessel"), which would instill a mystical power upon it. A good enough glyph maker could make a gun never run out of bullets or draw monster tattoos that came to life and killed people.

But this glyph was a Mona-fucking-Lisa.

Mr. Jaughter created a miniature town, complete with its own forest and sky. Then he mystically embedded it within an object. Whatever that object was, folks typically needed a triggering phrase to act as the key. This was how the Blood Furs managed to lose our surveillance; they kept leaving our world for their mystical sanctuary. Based on Gieter's stolen memories, there were a few hundred furballs inside. The scary thing was that they only needed to be within a few miles of the vessel for the triggering phrase to "bring" them in.

I gave Jaughter a farewell wave and nodded to Gieter, who shot him twice in the forehead. She inhaled deeply as his soul's memories flowed into her like a favorite scent. My partner's scowl deepened.

"Well?" I asked.

"Their vessel's a graffiti-covered door behind an abandoned gas station."

Cool. All we had to do was destroy it. Destroy the vessel and you destroy the pocket dimension. Anyone inside would just cease to be. It wasn't as much fun as mowing them down. But it would do quite nicely.

"Which town? Salem?"

Gieter nodded and gave me an eager, hate-filled smile.

"One more thing: Jaughter was bait."

Twelve werewolves erupted from the sand and roared at us under the Malibu sun. They had us surrounded. They were huge and dangerous. Each one of them probably had super powers.

I pitied them.

"Notify HQ," I muttered as I handed Gieter my gun and began to change. "We'll need a spin team at this site in a hurry."

So much for my new suit, which ripped apart as reptilian wings shot out of my back and flexed. The necromancer tucked our guns away and reached for her cell phone as I morphed and grew to my true size. She knew that I wouldn't crush her if she stayed put.

Besides, my silvery scales would protect her from pretty much anything. As the Blood Furs realized what I was, they turned and ran for dear life.

I exhaled flame and watched four of them burn.

When a bunch of mutated, silver-resistant werewolves kill and eat a heavily-armed FBI strike team, Washington doesn't send two regular agents. Instead, a pair of bruisers get called up and sent forth to make examples (and maybe a few fur coats) out of those responsible. Yeah, the Secret Service had other field agents with useful abilities. But they needed two agents who were immune to a werewolf's bite and could take a mauling . . . like us.

Besides, Gieter was good for getting quick answers from her victims. Being a necromancer, she was already dead . . . and thus harder to put down than most field agents. As for me, I was good at large body counts and immune to most things. Being an Afro-Chinese dragon, I was more than up for the task of killing white supremacists.

I'd capture one or two of them for the alchemists to poke at, but the rest would burn. As I completed my transformation, one of the werewolves actually started to fly away like Superman. Amused, I snatched the super beast out of the air with my clawed right hand, lifted him/her to mouth level, and then cut loose with a nasty torrent of dragon's fire. The stench of charred lycanthrope made my mouth water.

Too bad I gave up red meat last year (cholesterol).

THE PUPPET

They had me dead-to-rights on a moonlit night. Six plain-clothed Iranian spec ops troops surrounded me with assault rifles aimed at my head. Disguised as oil workers, they were so close that I could smell their collective, sweaty stench. I dropped my digital recorder, raised my hands, and slowly assumed a kneeling position. One of them ripped off my Ghillie suit, which exposed my desert fatigues. Since I had been lying prone in a patch of real bushes all night, they shouldn't have spotted me.

I slipped into the valley sixteen hours ago and uploaded damned nice footage of six well-camouflaged missile silos in the middle of a small, fake oil field. Their silos (disguised as oversized oil derricks) were surrounded by real ones. While the remote facility had been logged since its construction in the early 90's, no one had figured out it was fake until just last week. Some bored NSA egghead had been testing spy satellite upgrades and needed a map reference.

This location was picked out of a proverbial hat and the upgrades were tested. But instead of finding oil deposits, said upgrades picked up something else. He spotted well-shielded nuclear emissions, each some two hundred feet below the surface. They also had an underground pipeline that fed oil from another (real) oil field some ten miles to the southwest.

Higher-ups were notified and I ended up skydiving out of a modified stealth bomber two days ago. I hunkered down by day and hiked by night. I reached the target zone last night, dug myself in, and broke out my recorder/directional microphone.

As luck would have it, I picked up verbal chatter from two of the "oil workers" (streamed to Langley in real-time). Basically, a middle-aged major was getting a tour of the place from a guy in his late-50's, who he once referred to as "general." Through my camera, I could see that both men packed pistols under their work clothes. They also weren't afraid to speak freely.

What they said scared the shit out of me.

During the early '80's, a rogue group of Russian generals and high-level KGB officials came up with the insane idea of stashing thirty-five nukes throughout Iran. The smallest ones were in the six-kiloton range. The largest were twenty megatons. Some were stashed in hidden silos. Others were stored in secret bunkers near Iran's borders, where they could be trucked into other countries and detonated near key strategic sites.

These Russians—idiots that they were—figured that, should World War III start, it might be necessary to indirectly attack American allies and/or military bases in the Middle East. They recruited equally rogue elements within the Iranian military, who kept this secret from their own leaders.

The Iranian general expressed his utter amazement that this secret survived the fall of the Iron Curtain. Scarier still was the fact that the same Russians had all but given Iran the detailed breakdown for making nuclear weapons. If they wanted to, the Iranians could mass-produce them within a matter of months. Instead, their nuclear facilities were actually being used for peaceful energy production . . . and to prompt Israel into a pre-emptive strike.

Unfortunately, the Israelis didn't take the bait. Also, claimed the general, their intelligence suggested that the Israelis didn't know about these nukes. I had to agree. Otherwise, they'd have gone after them by now—with our help. After all, the Israelis would need help to go find and dismantle dozens of nukes, stashed all over Iran. They would've come to us. With my background, I'd have been tasked to one of those ops. Apparently, continued the general, his superiors had grown tired of this military-diplomatic shell game. More radical than their predecessors, they opted to simply take out Israel with some of their '80's-era stockpile. When the major voiced his concerns about Israel's ability to counter-launch, the general grinned and explained that the nukes wouldn't be launched from Iran. Oh no, explained the general, seven nukes *were already inside Israeli territory.*

They were strategically placed during the late '90's. Once the bombs went off, the Jewish state would cease to be. Since the nukes would have a Russian blast signature, Iran could not be blamed because they didn't have a nuclear weapons program. The Russians would probably conclude that some aging nuclear stockpile had been stolen by terrorists.

Best of all, the current regime didn't know about this conspiracy either. Thus, Iran's political leaders would publicly deny involvement and privately wonder what the hell happened. Western intelligence services would monitor their communiqués and absolve them of any blame, simply because they weren't in the loop. Thrilled by the possibilities, the two praised Allah and continued the orientation tour.

I was about to radio Langley for instructions when my motion sensor went off. Six blips were closing in on my position. While I was armed and not too averse to a quick shoot-out, I knew that I couldn't kill them all and get away. So I chose to press the button on a time-delayed charge that I had strapped to my chest harness.

Roughly the diameter of a dinner plate and four inches thick, the metal construct functioned much like a suicide vest. It was packed with a half-pound Semtex charge that would turn me—and this pack of shitheads—

into a smoking crater. The blast would happen in about thirty more seconds. I forced myself to pretend to be surprised and wished Langley the best of luck. Hopefully, they'd figure out how to stop these fucks without a global Armageddon.
Then the bastards caught me.

Now, I was lying prone in the dirt with my wrists being flex-cuffed behind me. One of the soldiers spotted my bomb, guessed what it was, and pulled out a knife. Unable to stop him, I could only watch as he cut the bomb loose. Even worse, the bastard had one hell of a throwing arm. He whipped the explosive like a pro Frisbee master and yelled for everyone to hit the dirt. My bomb exploded with tremendous, harmless, force.

As dry dirt and pebbles rained down, the guards rose to their feet. I earned a kick to my ribs for that little stunt. Alarms and shouts arose from the fake facility as the guards pulled their stashed AK's and ran to their action stations. Hidden searchlights flared to life and illuminated the darkened landscape. I wished I had a suicide tooth. It beat being taken alive inside of Iran.

Odds were I'd be tortured for everything I knew, paraded in front of CNN, and then executed. The guards turned off my gear and gathered it up. I'd happily tell them that their evil scheme had been compromised. They'd have to abort or risk an all-out retaliation from Israel, who might launch pre-emptively, once the CIA warned them. While I didn't see myself as a martyr type, I could take quiet pleasure in knowing that I might've saved millions of lives.

"*Please be quiet,*" an irritated woman's voice ordered . . . from inside my head?!
She had a familiar accent—

"I'm Israeli," she interrupted. *"And again, shut up with the inner monologue! You're thinking too much."* As the guards picked me up, I forced out a cleansing breath and tried to ignore the pain in my ribs as I emptied my thoughts.

"Much better," she said with a hint of praise. *"Please keep your eyes on the general or the psi-link won't hold."*

I obeyed.

A trio of jeeps raced toward my position, with four troops each. One of them carried the undercover general. Two of my captors dragged me between them as I kept my eyes on the fucker.

"Perfect," she purred. *"I'm glad your Russian's still good, Agent Verden. Follow my lead and I'll have you out of here before dawn."*

Russian? Okay, I'll play along. As the general stepped out of the jeep with an evil smile, I felt a rush of energy pass out of me, almost like an electrical current. The stoutly built general walked up to me and gently punched me in the right arm.

"Let him go," the general ordered in his native tongue. "Tell the men to stand down. This was a drill."

I fought the urge to gawk in shock. The guards quizzically regarded him for a moment before releasing me. One of them cut my flex-cuffs off with a knife. Another guard picked up a radio and called in the "all-clear."

"Men, let me introduce you to Anatoly Vasadrev . . . a 'friend' from Moscow. His specialty is in covert surveillance."

Oh, she was good!

I haven't used my Vasadrev alias in years, back when I was posing as a freelance assassin/information dealer. I had ties with Hezbollah, Hamas, and even Al-Qaeda. With a bit of luck, my cover might still hold up to casual scrutiny. The guards, who had clearly known too much about Russia's secret pact with Iran, exchanged grins.

I was in fucking awe. That psychic bitch wasn't in my head anymore . . . she was in the general's! Apparently, she commandeered his brain. If she could read my memories so well, then she'd surely do the same to the general.

He wouldn't know everything about this conspiracy. But he'd have to know something: names, dates, where the nukes were planted . . . enough for the Israelis to perhaps save their country from obliteration.

Hell, I bet she could even send an encrypted e-mail from the general's office straight to some intelligence facility in Israel. The lady could get me out of the country with ease—even with an armed escort if she so chose. When the smoke cleared, and the general was no longer useful, she could leave him to face charges of treason—possibly with no recollection of what had happened.

"Come!" the general winked. "You're to be my honored guest for the evening. I'm looking forward to your detailed assessment of our security."

"I'd be honored," I replied in the local dialect, with a Russian twang. "And then you could tell me where I screwed up, no?"

THE MIKUTU

Father Edgar Jaisalu slowly regained consciousness.

The short, kindly Nigerian was in his early 60's with thinning white hair. He felt nauseous as if enduring a hangover from his wilder youth. He was also very nearsighted. But even without his glasses, Jaisalu realized that he was tied to a metal chair in a frigid, dark room with a solid concrete floor. He also noted that his kidnappers left him in his Pittsburgh Steelers pajamas with nothing on his wrinkled feet.

The last thing he remembered was having a glass of goat's milk while grading a stack of papers in his bed. They must have drugged him. It would explain why he felt so–

A light switch was activated behind him and fluorescent overheads hummed to slow life.

"Hello, Father Jaisalu."

The priest didn't recognize the voice but could guess (by the accent) that he was dealing with an American.

"Hello?" Jaisalu replied in English, his mild accent laced with fear. "Who's there?"

A freckled, red-haired man walked into Jaisalu's line of view. Well into his 40's, he had a short, compact build with a surprisingly earnest face. In his right hand was a white mug of steaming hot coffee. In his left was a high-standing wooden stool. The American wore thick olive-drab trousers, a black turtleneck, and a brown bomber jacket. Most of all, the Jesuit noted his captor's black Desert Eagle .50 handgun, which hung heavily in its right hip holster.

"My name's Benjamin Truitt," the man began as he set the stool down with a guilty smile. "Please let me start by apologizing, for bringing you here like this."

"Uh . . . that's quite all right," Jaisalu replied with forced politeness.

"You're probably curious about why you're here."

"You could say that," nodded the priest.

Truitt set his cup on the stool, pulled Jaisalu's thick glasses from inside of his jacket, and then gently affixed them to the priest's face.

"Better?"

"Much," Jaisalu nodded as he rapidly blinked and took in his surroundings. The place had the feel of a storage room, with no windows or signs. Truitt picked up his cup and sat down.

"I'm here about a small tribe called the Mikutu," Truitt stated. Then he took a long sip of coffee.

Were Father Jaisalu white, he would've gone pale.

Mikutu was a small, remote village in the Horn of Africa, which had been massacred over twenty years ago. Almost every man, woman, and child had been systematically slaughtered. Of the 164 villagers, only three of them survived. Jaisalu had been delivering books to a nearby school when the trio stumbled out in front of his jeep—a wounded man being helped along by his wife and eight-year-old son. They begged him for a ride.

Naturally, Jaisalu drove them to the nearest clinic and contacted the authorities. Almost a full day had passed before the local police could reach the village. By then, the victims' bodies had been piled into a mass grave and burned beyond recognition. The perpetrators of the massacre left few clues behind—only the three surviving witnesses. When asked about the crime, the survivors said nothing, clearly too afraid of retribution. The father died during surgery. Before they could even bury him, his widow and son fled.

Their whereabouts were unknown to this day.

Eventually, the land was purchased by Randallson Oil. Soon after, the American-based corporation started drilling and "just happened" to discover oil where the village once stood. A refinery was built on the Mikutu's tribal lands and ended up becoming the source point of a lucrative pipeline. When Jaisalu contacted the Vatican about this horrid transgression, the Pope personally got involved.

The villagers of Mikutu had converted to Catholicism about thirty years ago. While the government didn't seem to care about punishing those responsible, the Catholic Church wanted justice. In time, what little evidence could be gathered pointed toward Randallson being behind the massacre. There were also hints that officials in the local government had been bribed. However, Randallson's legal team successfully thwarted all attempts to bring forth criminal charges, especially without any witnesses to testify.

In time, the case was closed and life went on.

"You work for them? For Randallson?" Jaisalu asked.

Truitt nodded.

"What is this about?"

"Eighteen years ago, someone began killing off Randallson employees. Each of the murders was . . . unique, bloody, and done by the same individual."

"How many have died?"

"105," Truitt stated, before taking another sip.

From the cover of a leafy tree, the lone Mikutu eyed the target area through the night vision scope of a suppressor-capped Dragunov sniper rifle. A leaf-covered mask concealed the killer's sweaty, deep-brown face as he counted Truitt's guards. He wore camo fatigues and an odd assortment of explosives, bladed weaponry, and infiltration gear.

Three hundred yards away was the small refrigeration plant where Truitt had taken refuge. One of the complex's three buildings was a small storage warehouse. The second (and largest) building used to process cheap, compact refrigerators. A few dozen yards away was a two-story building, designed much like a motel, which now housed Truitt's mercenaries.

Covered with broken windows, the office buildings had seen better days. Less than a month ago, Truitt had purchased the remote Nigerian facility and had secured it with the best security systems money could buy. The Mikutu studied the twelve exterior guards, five of whom were accompanied by leashed Dobermans.

"Go inside," the Mikutu commanded in a low voice, in the tongue of his dead tribe. "Tell me where the priest is."

The underbrush below him parted, as if an invisible someone being was running off to comply with his order. He patiently waited.

When one of the Dobermans stopped and began to bark, the Mikutu knew that his spy had crossed over onto the complex. The Doberman's handler stopped, raised his submachine gun, and looked around. Dressed in sand-colored fatigues, the white mercenary carried a light assortment of weapons and op tech. He looked competent and dangerous—but it didn't matter. As far as the lone Mikutu was concerned, this mercenary would die tonight, as well any of his comrades here . . . and especially Truitt.

But the priest had to be accounted for first.

Jaisalu had tried to see justice done for the slaughtered Mikutu and had thus earned mercy. Once the old Jesuit was safe, then he'd complete his blood vengeance.

Jaisalu's jaw dropped.

"You're saying that one person killed all of those people?!"

"Correct," Truitt grimly nodded. "Eighty of them had a military background. Most were warned to watch their backs. Some even hired bodyguards to protect them. But they kept on dying."

"What about the other twenty-five victims?" asked the priest.

"A half-dozen government officials and Randallson's board of directors."

"That's because they helped massacre the Mikutu, didn't they?" Jaisalu asked with open contempt.

"Yes," Truitt regretfully sighed.

"How many of you are left?"

"Just me," Truitt shrugged with a fear-laced smile. "I was one of the mercs who torched the village. I was just . . . 23 at the time. Our orders were to hit the place from all sides and kill everyone. I'm amazed those three villagers slipped past us."

"Oh God!" Jaisalu whispered with abrupt realization. "You think the boy is behind this?"

Truitt nodded.

"And you're going to tell me where he is, Father. After that, my men will deliver you home safe and sound. You have my word."

"Seeing as I know your face, your name, and the crimes you've done," Jaisalu countered, "I doubt you're going to let me live."

"What you know isn't important. What you can prove is," Truitt countered. "You won't be able to prove that you were kidnapped. And, frankly, you're smart enough to know what'll happen if you try."

Jaisalu glanced down at Truitt's sidearm and made his decision in an instant.

"I don't know where the villagers fled to. Even the Vatican couldn't find them. And if I did know where they were, I'd never tell you."

Truitt eyed the old priest for a moment

"This guy's coming to kill me, Father. I've got sixteen men watching this place. He'll kill them, too. I don't doubt it. You can prevent this."

"Why?" Jaisalu asked with a sneer. "So you and your thugs can get back to butchering innocent people? You sowed this, Mr. Truitt. Now reap it."

"Last chance, Father. Then I have to sit here and watch one of my guys work on you. He's something of an artist when causing people extreme pain."

Jaisalu stared ahead with resolute silence. Truitt pulled a small hand radio from his jacket.

"Send Hiers in," Truitt commanded.

"Copy that," a male voice replied.

As Truitt put his hand radio away, he suddenly stiffened. The merc dropped his coffee cup and spun about, gun drawn before the cup could smash against the cold floor. Jaisalu looked past Truitt and saw nothing. Yet, the mercenary's instincts screamed they weren't alone.

The Mikutu knelt at the base of the tree and shined a pen light on a patch of dark soil. An invisible finger drew out the layout of the facility—from the position of the interior guards to where Jaisalu was being kept. The Mikutu committed the diagram to memory and then turned off the pen light.

"Truitt's having the priest tortured," the spy said with a slow, hissing voice.

"Get the others," the Mikutu commanded. "I'll be inside shortly."

Jaisalu screamed.

Hiers knelt down in front of the priest. The sadist slowly—very slowly—cut through the flesh and bone of the Jesuit's left big toe with a small, hacksaw-shaped apparatus. The large Dutch mercenary was dressed like Truitt (minus the bomber jacket), with a 9mm pistol in his shoulder holster. A bag of torture implements rested on the floor.

As the priest's blood spurted onto Hiers' shirt, he completed the amputation. Even Truitt was a bit disgusted as the large mercenary picked up the bloody piece of Father Jaisalu and held it up for the priest to see.

"You should take better care of your feet," Hiers declared with a thick accent and a sick smile

Truitt turned away from the screaming priest, lit himself a cigarette, and checked his watch. With a muttered profanity, the aging merc pulled out his radio.

"Perimeter teams, you're overdue. Report."

The only response was static. Hiers looked up at Truitt as he nervously drew the Desert Eagle.

"Perimeter teams . . . report!" Truitt bellowed.

Again, nothing.

"Interior team—we've been breached. Fall back to my location. Do you copy?"

More static.

The door to the room was blown open. Jaisalu wasn't knocked back because his chair was bolted to the floor. Hiers wasn't so lucky. He half-drew his sidearm before the blast sent him sideways. As the weapon skidded from the sadistic merc, the Mikutu rushed in. Moving with trained grace, he sank a pair of small throwing knives into Hiers' neck with a one-handed throw. From his crouched perch in the corner, Truitt knew that the Mikutu hadn't seen him yet.

"To your right!" Jaisalu shouted, his ears ringing.

The Mikutu spun toward Truitt, another blade ready to throw, just in time to get shot in the chest. While the killer had body armor on, it didn't stop a fifty-caliber round. As the Mikutu fell to the floor, gasping for air, Truitt cautiously crept up with a two-handed grip on his weapon. He glanced through the empty doorway, saw that the killer was alone, and then relaxed.

After all, he had won.

"Finally got you, you sonuvabitch!"

An eager relief filled Truitt as he walked over to his victim, aimed for his torso, and emptied the clip. By the time the last shot thundered through the small room, the Mikutu lay dead at his feet.

Truitt knelt, triumphantly pulled the mask off, and blinked in surprise. The corpse was not that of the village boy, who would've been in his late 20's by now. No, the dead face he gazed upon belonged to a man in his late 40's.

His face was covered with wrinkles and old scars. Even in death, it held a quiet dignity. Truitt looked up at Jaisalu. Judging from the old Jesuit's equally-confused expression, he figured that the priest didn't know him either—

Suddenly, Truitt was knocked to the floor.

A pair of strong hands grabbed him by the waist, from behind. Another pair grabbed his left arm. Another pair grabbed him by the right arm and disarmed him. And a fourth pair seized his legs. Jaisalu couldn't see them at first.

But then they appeared before him—a roomful of transparent ghosts. All of them were black Africans. Most of them wore Western-style clothing. A few wore their tribal garb. Truitt squirmed in the grip of eight male ghosts, who quickly lifted him over their heads. The mercenary looked down at them and screamed hysterically as he realized who they were.

"No! We killed you!" Truitt yelled with a trembling voice. "I remember your faces! We fucking killed you!"

Without a word, the eight ghosts marched Truitt out of the room. A few more walked over to Hiers' bag, grimly pulled out assorted sharp objects, and followed them out. Most of the remaining ghosts surrounded their fallen avenger and silently mourned him. Then four male ghosts reverently picked up their slain champion and carried him away.

A young girl picked up Hiers' blood-covered saw and severed Jaisalu's bonds.

"You're all Mikutu?" Jaisalu winced as he took off his pajama top and started to rip it apart to bandage his foot.

One of the village elders approached Jaisalu with a kind smile.

"Yes," the ghost replied in broken English. "We came for our revenge."

"And that man was a Mikutu?"

"Yes," the ghost replied. "Omambu left our village when we converted to Catholicism. He believed in the Old Ways. When he heard what happened, he awakened our spirits. We helped him kill those responsible."

"What about the three villagers who got away?" Jaisalu asked, curious about their fate. "Where are they?"

The old ghost merely shrugged in reply.

IMMORTALITY

Isabella Dicontus abruptly awoke in the middle of a cool Seattle night.

Dressed in a short, red nightie, the busty brunette lay between the gray sheets of her king-sized bed. Slowly, the ivory-skinned beauty craned her head toward her closed bedroom door and listened. Her keen sense of hearing detected movement in the upstairs hallway, just outside. While Isabella couldn't see who it was, she could hear the hardwood floor creak under the weight of intruders.

Annoyed, she rolled her blue eyes toward the ceiling and reached under her thick pillows. Underneath was a black Heckler & Koch MP7. Affectionately nicknamed "Teddy Bear," Isabella never went to sleep without it. Just over two feet long, the submachine gun came with a night vision scope, six-inch sound suppressor, and was loaded with a 40-round magazine full of armor-piercing rounds. With more and more of her would-be captors wearing body armor, the tired cliché of sleeping with a mere pistol became impractical.

In fluid silence, Isabella rolled over the left side of her bed, putting it between her and the door. While there were two large windows leading into the room, she wasn't worried about someone crashing through the bulletproof glass. If someone did manage to breach them, she had plenty of surprises under her bed. Isabella thumbed the subgun's fire selector to "full-auto" and aimed for the door as moonlight poured in through the window behind her. While her skin would stand out, she wasn't too concerned about mere bullets.

On cue, a black-garbed man swiftly kicked the door open with a flashbang grenade in hand. His intention was to roll it in and withdraw. Instead, Isabella's four-round burst took his right throwing hand clean off. The intruder tumbled back, howling as the grenade rolled back into the hallway. Isabella ducked behind the bed, dropped her MP7, and slapped both hands over her ears with an evil smile. The flashbang went off with a blinding flash and deafening blast. A chorus of male screams filled the hallway.

With practiced efficiency, Isabella rolled over the bed with Teddy Bear. Her bare feet gracefully carried her into the doorway, allowing her a clear line of fire on four temporarily-stunned (and one dying) kidnapper. She gunned them all down with short bursts and no regrets. Then she paused to size them up through her weapon's scope.

Dressed in black, they each packed lightweight Kevlar vests, night-vision goggles, flashbang grenades, and tranquilizer pistols. Isabella used the corpses like stepping stones, allowing her to move down the hallway without slipping on their blood. She expected more than a five-man team (another reason why she didn't use pistols anymore).

Downstairs, three more black-clad men rushed into her loft's tastefully decorated living room. Armed like the bodies upstairs, they raised their tranquilizer pistols and fired. Isabella returned fire without hesitation, mentally cursing herself for not grabbing a spare clip from under the bed (or any frag grenades). The rush of a good "shoot-'em-up-up" had overridden her better judgment.

The MP7's clip emptied out as the last intruder fell dead on her expensive Persian rug. Isabella was surprised by the good fortune until she noticed a stinging sensation. With an annoyed sigh, she looked down and noticed a bright orange dart in her stomach. Even as she pulled it out, Isabella felt a sudden wave of weakness slip through her from the legs up.

Then, nothing.

* * *

Coming to, Isabella was still in her nightie. She was also chained to a red, ceiling-level support beam by both wrists. Her captors didn't just let her hang there. No, her legs were completely encased in freshly-dried cement. The amount of time it would take to set her up like this implied that Isabella had been unconscious for a long while.

Isabella figured the tranquilizer used on her was mystical in origin. Conventional chemicals—even poisons—rarely bothered her anymore. The metallic room looked like a cabin on a civilian freighter of some kind. The captive figured that she was either out to sea or about to be. Seeing as she had cement overshoes on, things looked pretty grim. In these situations, Isabella did what she always did.

She schemed.

After an uncomfortable few minutes, a door opened and in limped an elderly fellow. In his late sixties, he leaned on an ornate mahogany-and-platinum cane. He wore a gray three-piece suit with a gold Rolex on his left wrist. His skin was a sickly pallor and his white hair was receding.

"Good," he smiled with a raspy voice. "You're finally awake."

"And you are?"

"Herbert Faversham," the old man replied with a slight nod of the head. "Please allow me to apologize for the manner in which you were transported."

Isabella allowed herself to feign anger at being kidnapped—even though it happened at least once every few years.

"I'm not," she scowled. "Your triggermen got what was coming to them. Just name your ransom and be damned!"

"Your money doesn't interest me, Ava Vitallia," Herbert said, using her real name. "I want your secret."

"My secret?" Isabella coyly replied. "Which one? My mushroom soup recipe?"

Herbert sat in a nearby chair and rested his chin on the cane with a weary smile.

"Immortality," Herbert said with a hint of impatience. "I'd like to know how you achieved it."

"What the hell are you talking about?" she balked.

"Before you start lying about how you're just a normal woman, let me assure you that I've done my homework on your colorful past. Originally born in Madrid, circa 1831, you were the youngest of five daughters. You married and had three children. On December 6th, 1863, you died of pneumonia."

"You're insane," Isabella stiffly replied.

No matter how well she kept covering her tracks, someone always managed to track her down.

"Perhaps," he smirked. "Even though your mausoleum is quite empty. I also found numerous photographs of you in more recent years."

Herbert reached into his jacket and produced an old photo of her sitting at a table with Humphrey Bogart in the early 1950's. There was no doubt that it was Isabella.

"I've tried dozens of mystical cures, but the tumor in my brain just won't go away," Herbert explained. "When my sources told me about you, I knew you would be my salvation. I'm willing to offer you 50 million Euros—if you make me immortal."

"But I'm not immortal!" Isabella lied. "If I were immortal, the last thing I would be is a divorced socialite hanging around Seattle! I'd be doing something more meaningful; like working on world peace or ending hunger in poor countries. To live eternally—in our

hedonistic age—just wouldn't be worth the time . . .
even if such a thing was possible."

"I disagree with that last part," Herbert smiled as he
drew a .38 snub-nose from inside his suit jacket.

Isabella's eyes widened as he promptly shot her
twice in the forehead. Immediately, two burly men
rushed into the room with their machine pistols drawn.

Herbert handed the revolver to one of his men.

"Notify me when she revives," he commanded
before limping away.

Five minutes later, the bullets in Isabella's skull
were pushed out through the very wounds they just
made. As the wounds closed, Isabella slowly came to
with a disoriented groan of pain. One of the guards
noticed and went looking for Herbert. Isabella was
annoyed to find herself covered with blood and still
chained/half-cemented. Herbert entered with a clever
grin, just as the pain from Isabella's wounds abruptly
ceased.

"Now that we all know you're immortal, I was
hoping that you thought about my generous offer."

"If I refuse?" she asked.

"It would be a true shame if you sank to the bottom
of the Pacific."

Isabella examined the cement and sighed.

"Know any languages?" she asked, out of the blue.

Herbert frowned, surprised by the question. "What
does that matter?"

"It matters a great deal," she replied. "Do you
know any languages?"

The billionaire indulged her with a weary nod.

"French, German, Spanish, Chinese, and some
ancient Greek," he replied.

"Impressive," smiled Isabella. "Now, chisel me loose and release me after I make the elixir. I want half that money wired to my accounts now."

"Deal," Herbert replied, softly clapping his hands with a suppressed glee.

One henchman untied her while the other one left the room.

"I'll need ingredients," Isabella cautioned. "By the time you find them all, it might be too late."

"Not to worry," he assured her. "My ship's cargo hold's been converted into something of a laboratory. Most of the known alchemical ingredients in the world are at your disposal. You'll start immediately, yes?"

Isabella nodded. The other henchman returned with a jackhammer attached to a long hose. Herbert left the room and covered his ears as the jackhammer was placed against the cement block. Once freed from her restraints, Isabella was unchained and allowed a quick shower.

Her captors provided her with a white t-shirt, a pair of sweat pants, a gray lab coat, and a small pair of white slippers. Then, a pair of Herbert's gunmen led Isabella down to the cargo hold. True to his claim, Herbert had an impressive setup.

Some of the lab components were old-school tools while others were high-tech. There were dozens of shelves in the enormous hold. Combined, they held tens of thousands of alchemical ingredients—all alphabetized. Isabella slipped on a transparent lab visor and a pair of black rubber gloves. Four more armed men guarded this room and its very expensive contents.

"The money's been wired to one of your Swiss accounts," Herbert announced as one of his men showed her a tablet with the transaction details.

"Fair enough," Isabella replied, wondering if the data was real or faked.

While she had never met Herbert, the immortal knew his type—an untrustworthy old miser who'd break a deal faster than he'd honor one.

"How did you come across the formula?" Herbert asked as he sat on a stool next to her.

"I thought you knew everything about me," Isabella teased as she reached for a rune-covered bowl and weighed it carefully in both hands.

"I never said everything," he replied with a sly grin.

"That secret you'll never know," Isabella said with certainty. "Now, could someone fetch me some gold dust and a quarter-pound of troll liver, please?"

Herbert and his six gunmen watched Isabella use everything from a stone hammer to a centrifuge to a microwave oven. The ten-hour process concluded as Isabella slowly poured a honey-like substance into a cognac glass and set it on a table.

"I need a hair from your head," Isabella plainly stated as she took off her gloves.

Herbert leaned his head forward with a polite grin. "If you'd do the honors?"

Isabella ran her left hand through his hair and then plucked one. She regarded it for a moment and then carefully dropped it into the brew. As his hair disappeared into the potion, it glowed with a faint golden light. Herbert grinned expectantly.

"Done," Isabella wearily sighed.

"Are you certain?" Herbert asked.

Isabella gave him an annoyed stare. "Drink it down. It loses its potency within minutes."

"Then we'd better hurry," Herbert replied with a cunning grin, as he snapped his fingers.

Behind her, one of the gunmen approached Herbert and pulled a small box from his right pocket. He slung an M-4 assault rifle along his shoulder. Then he opened the box to reveal a small, sickly-looking white lab rat. It was laying on its right side and barely moved as Herbert gently pulled it out with his right hand. Isabella regarded the animal and realized Herbert's plan.

"I would've used a guinea pig," Isabella joked with a frown.

"My friend, Camille, could probably use your fine elixir more than me," Herbert grinned as he gently lowered the lab rat's whiskered mouth to the potion. The rat weakly lapped up some of the elixir before being pulled away. He then set the lab rat on the table and regarded Isabella with a sneer. The immortal folded her arms, knowing full well what would happen next.

Within a minute, the lab rat hopped up and began to move on its own with renewed youth and vigor. Herbert's jaw dropped with awe.

"As promised," Isabella replied, glancing up at a wall clock. "But you only had enough ingredients to make this one potion. It's getting stale as I speak. So, are you going to drink it or—?"

The immortal fought back a chuckle as the old man rushed to the table and greedily quaffed the potion down. Some of it dribbled down his chin as he emptied the glass. His tongue snaked out and collected the excess.

"How do you feel?" Isabella asked.

Herbert heavily exhaled.

"There's a—a warmth in my chest," he suddenly smiled. "Like I'm tingly all—"

A hundred steel blades suddenly erupted from his skeleton and shot out through his organs, skin, and clothes. Some blades were straight while others were serrated and still others were curved. Not a single drop of blood seeped from the wounds. The billionaire's minions gasped with a horrified shock that rivaled his own. Herbert's agonized brown eyes widened as they slowly turned milky white.

"Kill everyone else on this boat," she whispered to him in fluent, ancient Greek.

As Herbert Faversham fell over dead, Isabella arched her back, picked up the rejuvenated lab rat, and headed for a door with an exit sign over it. The six gun-toting henchmen swapped glances, unsure of what to do.

"Hold it right there!" shouted the gunman with the M-4.

He quickly unslung the weapon and rushed over to Herbert's corpse and dropped to a knee. Unable to safely check his employer's pulse, he glared up at her. Isabella half-opened the door and turned to face them as she stroked her new pet.

"The stuff in this room's worth tens of millions of dollars. Hock it, split the loot, and retire. What's the problem?"

"You killed our boss," growled the henchman.

"News flash: your boss kidnapped me, shot me in the head, and threatened to sink me to the bottom of the ocean! He had it coming."

"Get back here and fix him," the henchman growled, as he raised the M-4 to eye level and aimed it at Isabella. "If you know how to kill him, then you can bring him back to life!"

Isabella regarded the loyal henchman with a weary grin.

"Who says he's dead?" she winked.

Herbert's muscles suddenly expanded to the point where he had gained an extra 250 pounds of muscle and two feet of height. Worse, the blades were still extended. The monstrosity appeared to be the unholy union of a body builder and a knife rack.

The "immortal" gasped and then suddenly opened his all-white eyes with a vicious scream of madness. The lead henchman looked relieved—only to get a spike-covered fist driven through his torso. Herbert stood up with fluid ease and flicked the large corpse off his gore-covered fist.

The remaining gunmen forgot about Isabella, who exited the room as they opened fire on their employer. But their bruising gunfire bounced off Herbert's skin like rice off steel. His maddened eyes narrowed as he systematically stalked them all.

Isabella waited in the hallway until the screaming and shooting ceased. Then, she heard the heavy tread of Herbert as he entered the hallway. Covered in blood, blades, and tattered clothing, he glared down at her.

For a moment, she could see a spark of resistance in his eyes, mixed with downright hatred. If given the chance, he'd happily tear her apart. Unable to resist her command, Herbert roared in futile rage before racing off to dispatch the rest of the crew.

"Good doggy," she mocked.

THE BIRTHDAY FEAST

God damn me.

Those words go through my head every time I watch Gordon feed on another child. Today was special. Eight hundred years ago, this monster was born. To mark the occasion, my master sent me on an errand to snatch eight children. They were all between the ages of six and twelve—five boys and three girls. I tied them up in the basement cooler of an out-of-business butcher shop.

Their hands were bound together by strips of common nylon rope, which allowed me to suspend each one from a ceiling-mounted meat hook. I used the same type of rope to tie up their ankles. Each child was bound and gagged with white cloth, so that Gordon could enjoy feeding without being disturbed by his little victims' shrill screams. At present, the children futilely struggled, their whining muffled by their gags. They were upper-class, which Gordon usually requested because of their "superior flavor."

Via the light of a battery-powered lantern, I checked my watch. It was 11:28 p.m. and Gordon would arrive any minute. If he found the children to be suitable, he'd feed. Then, he'd pay me and leave. I'd take the money and get high for a few months. I didn't need the needle to relieve my conscience . . . I just needed the needle.

Once the heroin and the cash ran low, the entire process would begin anew.

Sometimes, he wanted whores. Other times, he had a taste for clergy. I know that I wasn't the only servant who fetched bodies for Gordon. There were others in every major city. While he said little about his other servants, I'm sure they were probably just as fucked up. Once I kidnapped his "menu," I'd find a quiet place for him to feed and set up a meet.

My direct employment commenced when the previous servant (and my mentor) had a change of heart. Barney was a kind, aging drunk who needed my junkie muscle for Gordon's errands. The poor fool went from fetching the menu to being on it when he had a crisis of conscience and refused to kidnap a pregnant mother. I torched Barney's remains and snatched up two pregnant women—as a peace offering. Gordon was so pleased that he gave me Barney's cut, in addition to my own.

Footsteps approached from behind.

Very nice, Gordon's velvety voice rasped inside my mind.

Gordon rarely uttered an audible word. While he claimed that he wasn't a vampire, Gordon would never tell me what he was. He said some secrets should never be shared. I could understand that. He was dressed in his usual style: expensive black suit, white shirt, no tie, and a diamond-encrusted gold watch on his left wrist. He stood a full head taller than me, with all-white hair. The suave monster looked to be in his late forties, with broad shoulders and a powerful build. While he wasn't a pretty boy, Gordon's intimidating, old money looks were regal enough to get him laid after a few drinks. Oh, and he's much stronger than any normal man. Hell, when Gordon was done "eating" Barney, he chucked the poor bastard across a twenty-foot room and cracked a wall in the process.

For you, Gordon grinned as he handed me a super-thick wad of cash.

"T-Thank you!" I stammered as I flipped through the mixed bundle of fifties and C-notes. There must've been about fifty grand in my hands—about three times his normal payout! Gordon walked up to his row of victims and chose the youngest boy. I was too busy counting to watch as Gordon fed. I'd seen it before and stopped trying to figure out how he did it.

With but a touch against a victim's skin, Gordon could drain a poor bastard's life energy away. It took about twenty seconds to suck the life from a child . . . maybe forty for a full-grown adult. The end result was always the same. He'd leave a shriveled-up, gray-skinned corpse with his/her face frozen in a mask of utter agony.

By the time I counted out the $48,250 bucks in my hand, Gordon had fed on all five of the boys. The blindfolded girls were freaking out and screaming through their gags as loud as they could. I looked up as Gordon gently pulled off the youngest girl's blindfold and placed both hands on her chubby little cheeks. The girl convulsed as Gordon fed; his eyes fluttering with ecstasy. Afterward, the girl's shoes had fallen to the floor, a direct result of her feet shrinking a size or two.

Better than the finest wine, Gordon's voice purred in my head. *Truly a shame.*

"What's that?" I asked, suddenly concerned.

"You got sloppy," Gordon said aloud as he moved to feed upon the second-youngest girl.

"I-I did what you said. What I always do," I countered, my voice shaking. "I took 'em all without leaving a trail!"

Gordon didn't answer. My only chance was the Glock 9 hidden beneath my coat. But he wasn't human. Ruining his clothes might only piss him off. Gordon turned to feed on the second girl. After she was dead and shriveled, he pointed toward the last girl.

"For what I'm paying you, I expect my meals to be more carefully screened."

I wanted to ask Gordon what he meant but I was too scared to talk.

"Her stepfather's a senior FBI agent," Gordon revealed. "Granted, you did manage to kidnap her from school without incident—a truly impressive feat, by the way. But with his resources, I'm fairly certain he'll find you."

"I'll leave town," I shrugged, my heart pounding as I pocketed the money. "If you don't want me around, I'm gone."

Gordon turned and slowly headed toward me with that damned regal smile on his face. I backed away as my left hand strayed toward the gun. Gordon smiled as though he had read my thoughts. My heart skipped a beat as my back met the wall. He stopped a few feet away from me and held out a hand.

"Please dispose of the bodies, as usual. It was a pleasure having you in my employ, Daniel."

I stared down at his manicured hand, then back into his brown eyes. I shook his hand, expecting to end up like Barney. Instead, Gordon shook my hand firmly, patted me on the shoulder with his other hand, and headed for the door.

"What about the girl?" I asked.

"Dump her—alive—somewhere safe. Then come back and burn the bodies."

"D-Done," I managed.

Gordon waved farewell and left.

I ran over to my carrying case and pulled out a bottle of chloroform. Pouring some onto a handkerchief, I clamped it over the girl's mouth and waited. Within seconds she was unconscious. After I carefully removed her from the meat hook, I threw her into the trunk of a beat-up gray Toyota and drove her to the *Haven of Light* homeless shelter.

Lights were still on inside as I carried her across the street, left her at the door, and returned to the car. Then I picked up a large piece of dislocated asphalt and lobbed it through one of the front windows. By the time I got the car started and made it halfway down the street, the front door opened. It wouldn't matter if someone identified the Toyota. I stole it yesterday and had every intention of torching it on the way out of town.

But right now, all I had to do was get to the butcher shop and dispose of the bodies. Then it was off to some interstate motel, where I could tap my trusty needle and succumb to some much-needed sleep. I parked in the back and went downstairs with a can of kerosene.

The meat locker was lit when I left. Now, the whole place was completely dark. The lantern's battery was fresh and should have lasted all night. I dropped the kerosene and drew my gun. My right hand shook despite my best efforts to keep it steady.

God, I needed a fix!

"Gordon?" I called out, not wanting to go into the pitch-black room.

I'm so hungry, a boy's voice echoed in my mind.

Me too, a girl's voice added, also in my head.

Oh fuck no!

I turned and fled. But they were faster—just like their "father."

With frightening ease, all seven victims rushed out of the darkness and drove me to the floor. They ripped my clothes apart like wrapping paper and greedily put their hands on any bare skin that they could touch. Their combined feeding made me convulse so badly that I fired a wild shot into the darkness, before the youngest girl swatted the pistol away.

Gordon set me up! Before tonight, he always had me burn the bodies right after a feeding.

Now I knew why—

THE GUNNY

Gunnery Sergeant Ned Urlich emitted a soft groan as he slowly regained consciousness. Red alert klaxons blared as he surveyed the cramped interior of his white, coffin-shaped cryobed. In his late thirties, the grizzled marine had been in quarantine stasis since an exploration run on GS-453. An isolated swamp world near the galactic rim, GS-453's environment was toxic to human life but ideal for space armor drills.

Urlich was leading such a drill when he was swept off a low cliff by a rockslide. The half-mile fall didn't hurt him. But it did rupture the right shoulder seal on his armor. His men quickly patched the leak before the planet's toxic atmosphere could do real harm. Yet, he picked up a stubborn viral infection that the sick bay geeks couldn't identify or purge from his system.

As a result, Captain Yemtis ordered him tucked away in stasis until they could reach Delphi Station and get him properly detoxed. A glance at a wall monitor told Urlich that he'd been asleep for about two weeks. They should've been halfway there by now. The cryobed's seals self-unlocked, something it was not supposed to do without medical staff supervision.

"Computer," Urlich called out as he opened the stasis bed. "What's going on?"

"This is a ship-wide emergency," the ship's AI replied with a female voice. "Your assistance is required."

"Explain," Urlich yawned as he rolled out of the cryobed in his white patient's gown and bare feet. He wiped the sleep crud from his gray eyes and stretched his lean, 6'2" frame. Urlich's weary muscles made audible sounds as he felt the aching remnants of every injury he had earned after nineteen years of hard, devoted service to the Corps.

"A saboteur bypassed ship security and poisoned the water supply."

"How many dead?" Urlich asked, suddenly alert and worried.

"3,996 crewpersons."

A carrier-class ship, like the *Bismarck*, had a standard crew of about 4,000.

"You're saying I'm the only one left?"

"Correct."

"And this saboteur?"

"The crew managed to identify her before they succumbed to the poison. Unfortunately, they were not able to capture her alive."

"Any clues as to motive?"

"Affirmative," replied the AI. "Long-range sensors have detected twelve hostile vessels closing in on our position."

"What class?" Urlich asked.

"*Trojan Raiders.*"

Urlich sighed and began to pace.

He knew that only smugglers and pirates used *Raiders* these days. The ships were fifty years old and way too small to deal with a spacecraft carrier like the *Bismarck*. With a full crew, the *Bismarck* could take on fifty *Raiders* and probably win.

By himself, it wouldn't be so easy.

Even with the AI handling the defensive weaponry and thrusters, *Raiders* tended to carry swarms of fighters and boarding pods: too many for the *Bismark's* guns to take out. Without fighter support and marines to fend off boarding parties, the pirates could probably take the ship. They'd lose most of their ships and crew doing it.

But they'd still win.

Urlich wondered if the AI could take out the *Raiders* before they launched their ships. Perhaps some fancy maneuvering and long-range shooting could trim their numerical advantage.

"So what's the game plan?" Urlich asked. "While you're killing off their fleet, what do you want me to do?"

"The weapons are inactive, due to a shipwide systems virus."

"You neglected to mention that little detail," Urlich stopped and scowled. "How bad is the bad news?"

"We have lost communications and most of the other core system functions as well. Emergency power is at 49% and falling."

"Let me guess: we can't run away either?" Urlich asked as he resumed his pacing about.

"Affirmative," came the computer's reply. "The saboteur rendered our reactor drives inoperable. With a normal contingent of engineers, it would take 8.33 hours to repair."

Urlich headed for the door of his quarantine room, which slid open. Normally, it could only be unlocked by one of the med techs. But the computer bypassed the safety protocols. After all, with everyone else dead who could he possibly infect?

"ETA on incoming ships?" Urlich asked as he exited into a corridor and almost tripped over a dead crewman.

"6.54 hours."

Urlich sighed as he looked around. The corridor was littered with uniformed bodies—all pale with green bile on their lips. They couldn't have been dead longer than a few hours. Urlich crossed himself as he made his way toward his quarters.

"Why did you wake me?" he asked with growing frustration. "Just blow us up."

"Due to the virus, I cannot activate the auto-destruct."

Urlich reached an elevator, hit a button, and waited for it to arrive. He understood what duty required him to do. He had to destroy the *Bismarck* before it could fall into enemy hands. There was just one problem with this: he wasn't quite ready to die yet. In fact, he was about nine months away from retirement and his life dream of restoring vintage hovercars. The only thing he loved more than being a marine was fixing things.

As far as Urlich was concerned, there was a way out of this mess. He'd just have to figure it out.

"What's this AI virus do again?" Urlich asked as the elevator doors opened.

"Full-system shutdown," the computer replied. "Including artificial gravity and life support."

"How long until you're completely helpless?" Urlich asked as he stepped into the elevator.

"52.5 minutes. Are you headed for Engineering or toward the fighter bays?"

"My quarters," Urlich muttered. The elevator lights began to flicker as he pressed a button for one of the crew levels. "I'd rather die with my boots on. And turn that fucking siren off, would you?"

"Affirmative," the computer replied.

Exactly 10.21 minutes later, Urlich exited his quarters in full combat dress as he headed for the bridge. He couldn't think of a single way to avoid dying. If he hit the fighter bay, he could snag a heavy bomber and nuke the *Bismarck*. The problem with that plan was that he'd be stuck in deep space without enough fuel or air to make it to *Delphi Station* or any of the nearest colony worlds, which equaled a slow death.

The only bright spot Urlich could see to blowing up the reactor—from inside the ship—was that he might take a bunch of pirates with him. Or he could rig the ship with nukes, hop a fuel shuttle, and head home. While the shuttle was slow, it had enough fuel and life support to get him somewhere civilized. The only problem was that the pirates could catch up to him with ease. And because fuel shuttles didn't have weapons, that option sucked too.

Since escape wasn't feasible, the only fun thing to do would be to rig the ship with nukes, proximity mines, and maybe a dead man's switch. He could suit up in space armor, wait for the bastards to board and kill as many of them as he could—before they took him out. Once he died, the dead man switch would set off the nukes . . .

A stubborn part of him refused to accept any of these options. As Urlich headed for the armor bays, he passed an open door and heard Hendrix music blaring from within. Neo-Classical Earth music was pretty popular with the swabbies and jarheads—one of the few things they had in common. Urlich backed up and saw that one of the crewmen was slumped over his desk, halfway into a farewell letter. A portable music player—roughly the shape and size of a silver dollar— blared *Purple Haze*.

As Urlich bobbed his head to the music, something happened within his infected brain. A dozen new ideas suddenly came to him. The space marine cracked a hopeful smile.

"Computer," Urlich said as he left the quarters. "Don't you have a secondary AI core? I heard they're left uninstalled, in case of situations like this."

"Affirmative," came the reply. "However, the saboteur damaged it before she was killed. The engineering team managed to repair it but died before installing the unit."

"Could you talk me through it?" Urlich asked with sudden confidence.

"You are unqualified to install the unit. The probability of you successfully activating—"

"Shut up and start talking!" Urlich yelled as he moved on.

The computer began to talk. At first, it made sense. But once the gunny was out of earshot of the music, it abruptly sounded like the techno jargon he tended to ignore before his accident. He stopped, told the computer to pause for a moment, and then ran back into the range of the music. As he did, Urlich realized that everything the AI had said made sense again.

It had something to do with the music. Probably that damned swamp virus as well.

Strange, Urlich thought as he snatched up the music player and ran toward the bridge elevator.

Another dozen new ideas slipped into his brain along the way.

Another 15.3 minutes later, Urlich manned one of the bridge's systems stations and typed like a man possessed. Metallica's *Don't Tread on Me* blared in the background. Even the ship's computer had difficulty following what he was doing. At first, it thought he was attempting to prep the secondary AI core for installation. Then, it recognized that he was going after the AI virus.

Unfortunately, the techs on the *Bismarck* barely had time to discover its existence before they died. Even if the crew had survived, it was unlikely that they could've countered the systems virus in under a week—if ever. It was so far beyond state-of-the-art that even the AI itself couldn't begin to understand what Urlich was doing—

"Gotcha, bitch!" he triumphantly muttered.

Were it possible, the AI would've scratched its proverbial head. Somehow, its primary operating systems were returning to normal.

"How are you feeling?" Urlich asked the computer.

"Communications, weapons, and life support are all returning to normal," the AI replied. "Emergency power core has stabilized and begun recharging. However, the main reactor drives are still inoperable. Activating auto-destruct—"

"Whoa!" Urlich angrily interrupted. "Anybody ever tell you that you've got a fuckin' death wish?! C'mon! We don't need to die today!"

"The ship's engines are still down. Only maneuvering thrusters are operable, which will neither allow us to flee or adequately maneuver for long-range combat. Even if we could, I would be unable to repel all twelve enemy ships, their fighters, and boarding pods. Eventually, they would capture or destroy this vessel."

"I agree," Urlich replied with an evil smile. "So why even let them attack?"

The *Bismarck* came into view of the incoming pirate fleet. Their flagship, the *Rasputin*, was commanded by Captain Noah Vermes. A tall, brown-bearded man in his early forties, Vermes sat in his captain's chair with an eager look on his cruel face. A form-fitting black uniform hugged his muscular frame as he watched the Bismarck helplessly drift.

This was the haul of a lifetime: to capture a spacecraft carrier intact. The ship was stocked with enough armaments and supplies to keep his fleet running for at least three years. Then there was the ship itself—complete with its pair of fancy new AIs; either of which would net a fine sum on the black market. He already had buyers lined up, with the Interstellar Jihad offering the most money.

Frankly, Vermes wasn't too fond of selling to terrorists. But any sworn enemy of U.N. Command sat well with him. The idea of a bunch of neo-Muslim fanatics blasting the military with one of its best warships struck him as ironic.

"Launch fighters and boarding pods," Vermes ordered. "Once the ship's secured, send the dropships."

"Aye sir," replied one of his techs.

Within moments, Vermes could see the various cruisers launch their hundreds of fighter and boarding pod complements.

"Sir," another tech reported. "There's still one lifesign aboard."

"Is it our girl?" Vermes asked. He had placed a few wagers that his handpicked saboteur would still be alive. Arenda was a really good lay—not to mention one of his best "gremlins." The clever girl was probably waiting around in a spacesuit.

"Negative. The lifesign's male."

"It's probably someone in their sick bay," Vermes replied with a disappointed sigh. "Isolate the lifesign and notify the boarding parties to take him alive. Maybe he knows enough classified information to be a useful hostage."

That would sweeten the deal with our prospective buyers, Vermes thought.

"We're being hailed through the ship's main communications array," a third tech announced with a hint of worry in her voice

Vermes frowned. There was still one mobile crewmember that hadn't succumbed to the poison aboard his prize. What bothered him more was that the systems virus hadn't yet taken down the *Bismarck's* communications array, which should've gone down with the AI.

"Tell the fleet to activate shields and weapons," he stiffly ordered.

"Aye, sir," replied the female tech.

"Put him on-screen," Vermes commanded as he leaned back into his chair and put on his game face.

The image of Urlich appeared on the screen, still in his marine garb. He sat in the captain's chair, with his feet propped on Captain Yemti's balding corpse as if it was a footrest. Ulrich had a lit cigar in his mouth. Jay-Z's *Big Pimpin'* blared in the background.

Shit! Vermes thought to himself. He was hoping that he'd be dealing with a spineless ensign with a piss stain in his pants—not a fucking space marine!

"Hi," Urlich muttered as he exhaled smoke through his nose.

"Sir," announced the first tech. "The *Bismarck's* powering up. Shields, thrusters, and batteries are online."

Vermes sighed. *So much for the easy way*, he thought. Still, they could batter down the *Bismarck's* defenses and take the ship. But he'd lose half his fleet doing so. The value of his prize would shrink with every hull breach. Vermes wondered if this jarhead could see reason and make the smart play. A little polite bullshit just might win the day without a shot fired.

"Identify yourself," Vermes called out.

"Marine Gunnery Sergeant Ned V. Urlich," he replied with a smug grin.

"Sergeant's don't get paid much," Vermes pleasantly grinned. "Nor is it very likely that you're ever going to take on my fleet and win."

"Are you making me an offer?" Urlich teasingly asked.

"I'm open to suggestions," Vermes replied, knowing that he'd kill this son of a bitch the first chance he'd get.

"Well," Urlich whimsically replied. "How about you let me fly off in one of the *Bismarck's* fuel ships? I would, of course, raid the ship's Paymaster's Office on the way out. Then, once I feel safe, I'll tell you where I left the nukes."

"'Nukes?'" Vermes asked with raised eyebrows.

"Yeah," Urlich lied with pride. "Boobytrapped 'em myself after I activated the secondary AI core. Did I forget to mention that I'm a demo specialist?"

"Must've slipped your mind," Vermes thoughtfully replied.

He had bomb disposal teams capable of finding and disarming nukes. But the *Bismarck* was four miles long and two miles wide. And the marine had plenty of time to stash them throughout the ship and would know various ways of hiding them from detection.

"Sorry. I'm forgetful that way," Urlich shrugged. "Old age is creeping up on me. That's why I wanna retire early and disappear."

"One of the colony worlds?" Vermes asked. "Somewhere out past the Rim?"

The marine nodded.

A man of Urlich's skills could make a fine living in the frontier, especially if he worked freelance. Vermes glanced at a tactical monitor and realized that his fighters and boarding pods had just entered the *Bismarck's* optimal firing range.

"Do we have a deal?" Urlich asked. "Or do I get to have a little target practice before I die?"

"We have a deal," Vermes sighed. "We'll wait for you to launch before boarding."

Vermes signaled one of his communications techs to have his fleet ships, fighters, and pods stand down. He'd have to find those nukes before Urlich got out of the range of his fighters. While the nearest U.N. ships were two weeks out, he didn't want to any of the *Bismark's* crew to survive: especially this one.

"Very thoughtful of you," Urlich replied as he glanced at his watch and started to rise. Then, he sat down, as if he had just remembered something. "Wait a sec. I forgot to mention one more thing."

"What?"

"About that kickass systems virus . . ."

"What about it?" Vermes impatiently asked.

"Not that one," Urlich replied. "I was talking about my virus."

On cue, all of Vermes' fighters and boarding pods suddenly shut down. Each of his *Raiders* suddenly shut down three seconds later. Every system went offline—from life support to weapons to reactor cores. Vermes and his bridge crew suddenly found themselves afloat in a darkened bridge, minus their artificial gravity as well.

Vermes saw Urlich wave a middle-fingered good-bye, a split-second before the *Rasputin's* communications systems failed. Then it hit the pirate like a slap in the face. The bastard had a slipped a fast-targeting systems virus into the transmission! Worse, when Vermes gave the stand-down order, he had unwittingly infected all of his other ships.

Urlich's virus had somehow bypassed his fleet's anti-viral systems during their brief chat. It could take hours, perhaps days, for his fleet to get back up and running again. The pirate shook his head at the thought of being outsmarted by a jarhead with a taste for bad music. They'd probably give Urlich a chest full of medals for capturing a pirate fleet single-handed.

Vermes ordered his bridge crew to fish out the spacesuits and portable communications gear. They'd have to broadcast a surrender call to the bastard or risk being picked off like skeet. While Vermes didn't relish the idea of ending up in prison (again), the crafty villain was confident that he could escape (yet again), given time and planning.

The *Bismarck's* maneuvering thrusters suddenly flared to life. Vermes watched the warship move closer, well within easy firing range of his entire fleet. Then it came to a halt. Odds were that Urlich was merely flexing his muscles. Vermes listened intently as one of his communications officers sent a surrender signal, via one of the portable communications units.

"Signal acknowledged and surrender accepted," the officer replied.

Vermes breathed a sigh of relief.

For a moment, he thought that Urlich was actually going to open fire. A half-second later, the Bismark's four massive ion turrets turned the *Rasputin* into a ball of fiery debris.

On the bridge of the *Bismark*, Urlich drank out of a plastic beer can, with five other unopened cans laid out on a tactical console. Captain Yemti's corpse was respectfully re-positioned in his command chair, where the marine figured he belonged. The sergeant paced around the bridge, deep in thought. In the background, *Paint It Black*, by the Rolling Stones, was playing.

"There are regulations against killing prisoners, Sgt. Urlich," the AI noted. "Even in these circumstances."

"Yeah," Urlich agreed as he tossed the empty can aside. "Lucky for me I'm going AWOL before they court-martial me."

"Are you deserting because of your brain-enhancing virus?"

Urlich smiled. If the AI could put it together that quickly, so would U.N. Command. He could never go home again.

"That's right," Urlich admitted. "Once the brass figured out what it could do, they'd snatch me out of my prison cell and stick me in a lab. I'd spend the rest of my short, short life being vivisected. Once they figured out how to replicate it, the virus would just end up as one more weapon that the bad guys could steal."

"What is your plan?"

"We'll think of something. But for now, would you kindly kill each and every last one of these mother fuckers?" Urlich asked, as he grabbed another beer can and popped it open. "They're blocking my view of the cosmos."

"Affirmative," the AI replied.

The massive warship's missile batteries and ion turrets leisurely targeted the rest of Vermes' helpless fleet and opened fire.

LIES BECOME TRUTH

Tom Mayner woke to the insistent chiming of his doorbell at 6 a.m. on a Saturday morning. At thirty-nine, the chubby millionaire glared at his alarm clock and wondered who the hell was bothering them this early. Sarah, his blonde trophy wife, slept through the noise with little difficulty.

Dressed in yellow silk pajamas, he threw on his red terry cloth bathrobe with a scowl. Then he slid into his black leather slippers and headed for the door. Tom stormed across the second floor of his expensive suburban home, past the rooms of his children (Ron and Marie), and down a flight of stairs. The doorbell rang with every other step. Tom reached the front door and flung it open.

"What?!" he yelled, red-faced.

Vivian Ducher stood outside.

A year older than Tom, she was a half-head taller and skinny enough to vaguely resemble Olive Oyl, from the *Popeye* cartoons of old. Her black hair was streaked with strands of gray and combed back into a long ponytail which ran halfway down her back. She wore a pink, flower-patterned dress and had a worried expression on her unattractive, long-nosed face. Behind her was his brand-new gray Porsche, which was parked in his home's winding driveway. Tom narrowed his eyes with recognition.

"Stuttering Storky?!" Tom blurted out with a shocked smile. "Is that you?"

Vivian's eyes narrowed for a brief moment of ire. "Stuttering Storky" was a title slapped on Vivian during her high school days. Being tall, skinny, and ugly was bad enough. But her heavy stutter had made her life hell. The popular students—like Tom—relentlessly tormented her, even after she tried to kill herself with a razor during her sophomore year. During senior year, Vivian's parents pulled her from the school and Tom heard nothing more of her.

"Actually," she replied, without the stutter, "my name is Vivian."

She held out her right hand with a forced smile. "Good to see you again, Tom."

Out of reluctant politeness, Tom shook Vivian's hand. As he did, a strong burning sensation passed through his arm, as if he had placed his hand on a hot stove. Tom jumped back and looked down at his hand with surprise and concern. But his skin was unmarked and the pain had already faded away.

"Why are you ringing my bell at 6 a.m.?!" Tom asked with a downward frown at his hand.

"I just wanted to make sure you were all okay," Vivian lied with a sudden, eerie smile. "I heard you had run into a patch of bad luck."

"Me? Run into bad luck?" Tom chuckled as he looked at her. "I own the fifth largest accounting firm in the state. I'm married to an ex-model and have two awesome kids. And that Porsche behind you is mine.

Aside from my Benz being in the shop, my luck's better than good."

"Really?" Vivian asked. "I heard that you were about to be indicted for laundering money for some Panamanian drug cartel."

"Then you heard wrong!" Tom laughed.

"That's strange," she continued. "I heard that you did. And that you were skimming money off the top."

Tom was still laughing at the idea that he would do business with a drug cartel. His reputation for being squeaky clean was etched in stone. All of his accountants were routinely checked for signs of wrongdoing.

He always ran background checks on his larger prospective clients. If anyone even seemed to be linked to a criminal enterprise, he would simply avoid doing business with them and recommend a rival firm to better suit their needs. The notion of being a money launderer was too ridiculous for Tom to take seriously.

"And what else did you hear? Like, the Loch Ness Monster's coming to eat my cat?"

Vivian gave a nerdy little laugh in reply, which Tom found amusing.

"Well, I heard that your wife was sleeping with the guy across the street and that both of your kids aren't yours."

Tom's smile vanished, replaced with a sincere scowl.

"All right, Storky. It's time you leave."

Vivian nodded with a quiet anger.

"Fair enough," she conceded. "I just wanted to make sure you were all right. It's been good seeing you on your feet, Tom. Especially since your mistress gave you AIDS and everything."

"I don't have a mistress!" Tom yelled, as his face reddened. "Now get off my porch, you crazy bitch!"

Vivian's face sprouted that eerie smile again. With a parting nod, she turned and walked away. Tom slammed the door and went upstairs. He'd have to call Sid Conyez on Monday. The private investigator was so good he could find Bigfoot if someone paid him to. Sid would find out everything about Vivian and see what that psycho chick was up to. For now, Tom returned to his wonderful life and his comfortable bed.

The accountant enjoyed his weekend so much that he had actually forgotten about Vivian's bizarre visit.

As Tom arrived at his office, the following Monday, he found dozens of local cops and FBI agents on the premises. His files were being confiscated and eight of his brightest accountants were under arrest. Every local news network had a team in place, reporting on the raid. Tom was promptly arrested, Mirandized, and stuck in a holding cell with a pair of huge felons who thought he had a nice ass.

Having been properly beaten and molested, Tom limped to a pay phone to make his one phone call. When he dialed his loving wife, a man's voice answered on the other end.

"Who the hell is this?!" Tom yelled.

"Warren," the voice replied. "I live across the street."

"W-What are you doing in my house?!"

"I'm helping your wife move into my house," came Warren's smug reply. "When she found out you were laundering money for a drug cartel, she finally decided to leave your unfaithful ass."

"What are you talking about?! I never cheated on my wife!"

"You're full of shit," Warren replied. "Sid Conyez took some pretty disgusting photos of you banging some trailer-trash whore."

Tom's mind reeled. This wasn't possible! It had to be a setup . . . but how?!

"I promise to raise the kids as if they were my own, you spermless prick," Warren taunted, before hanging up.

Tom lowered the phone and stared off into space with amazement.

Four years passed.

Tom slept in the prison infirmary, a gaunt shell of his former self. He was divorced, penniless, and the children hated him. Five attempts had been made on his life by killers from a drug cartel he had never heard of. The only bright spot to his twenty-year sentence was that the prison had excellent facilities for treating terminal AIDS patients. But Tom didn't really mind dying. Having lost everything, he really couldn't wait for the Reaper.

"How are you feeling, Tom?" Vivian's voice asked from the other side of the room.

Vivian headed toward him in that same pink dress. Only now, Vivian looked like a teenager again! In shock, Tom looked around at the four other patients in the room. Two played cards. One slept. The fourth was writing a letter. The prison doctor passed right through her!

"I tried to find you," Tom weakly said. "When I heard you were dead, I just didn't believe it. Now it all makes sense. What'd you do to me? Some kind of curse?"

"You always were the smart one, Tom. That's why I asked you for help with Physics class. Remember?"

Oddly enough, he did. He remembered that Vivian was failing the class, swallowed her pride, and came to him for help. He offered to tutor her. Then, as a prank, he showed her flawed equations and basically set her up to fail her midterm exam. His buddies bought him a six-pack of beers for that one.

It seemed like a good idea, back then.

"When I failed Physics, my dad beat me so bad that I coughing up blood," Vivian sadly reminisced as she sat in a chair next to Tom's bed. "That's when I just gave up."

"What'd you do?" he asked.

"I swallowed a bottle of pills and died, Tom. My parents 'withdrew' me from school and didn't tell anyone."

Vivian's expression darkened as she remembered her early days as a ghost. "They just had me cremated, left my urn on the front porch, and blew town. The cheap fuckers didn't even have a wake!"

The ghost stared off with a vicious smile.

"But I came back, Tom—with powers. My parents? They were the first to die."

Tom looked down at his right palm and remembered the pain of that cursed handshake.

"I've been settling old scores ever since," Vivian said with a shrug. "At least my stutter went away."

Tom sank into his mattress and felt like slime.

"You lied to me about Physics, so I thought it fitting that I turned your life into a lie. The most amazing thing is that if you lie hard enough—I mean just right—you can bend reality."

Tom thought about apologizing but realized it wouldn't help. Nothing would. But something inside him refused to give up—even now. His mind searched for a solution.

"Well," Vivian said as she rose to leave. "I'm done with you. I think I'll pay Skip Hunt a visit. You remember him, don't you?"

"Wait," Tom painfully sat up. The other prisoners curiously looked at him, thinking he was talking to himself. "You can fix this!"

"I am 'fixing' this, you son of a bitch!" Vivian snipped. "I'm going to take out every last one of you. Maybe then I'll find some peace."

"No!" Tom begged. "Listen! If you can bend reality, can't you go back?! Back to those shitty years?!"

Vivian paused, surprised that she hadn't considered that possibility.

"You could lose the stutter, become the most popular girl in school, and make your dad a non-violent hippie—if you lied just right."

"But you'd just do what you did to someone else."

"True," Tom admitted, his voice thick with desperation. "But it beats being dead, right? You'd have your life back! You could have anything you wanted—right?"

Vivian glared at him, unsure if he was trying to deceive her (yet again).

But the rationale was so solid . . .

MY BOY

Cyrus DeClaire stepped off the stagecoach and surveyed the small town of Payne Ridge, Nevada. In his late fifties, the sunburned Cajun seethed with a quiet rage under the brim of his fancy gray hat. The matching gray suit, red vest, and ruffled white shirt gave him the look of a gambler/swindler who had just stepped off a riverboat. It was a guise meant to conceal his real intentions, which had nothing to do with money.

The Cajun adjusted his fancy gray gun belt and watched as both coachmen unloaded his two heavy black trunks. They had been well-paid to handle his luggage with the utmost care, under the not-so-subtle threat of a bullet if anything was broken inside. He spotted a nearby hotel and eyed the three-story building with a clear distaste. Once both trunks were safely on the ground, Cyrus pulled a thick roll of bills from inside his vest and handed some out.

"Check me into that hotel," Cyrus told the coach driver, his Cajun accent quite distinct. "I'll be along to collect the key."

"No problem, boss," replied the bearded driver, as Cyrus put way too much money into the man's calloused palm.

The new arrival ignored the intense afternoon sun and headed for the stable with grim resolve. Therein, he found a young kid tending horses. Cyrus explained he wanted to rent a horse for a day and asked if one could be spared. The kid told him that his pa had to make those decisions. Cyrus eyed the fifteen-year-old boy with a strange smile, dropped enough money to buy three horses into his hand, and then saddled up a decent white mare.

He then mounted the steed and asked for the location of the graveyard.

Twenty minutes later, Cyrus DeClaire had ridden his way up a low hill and found himself at the town's simple, sizeable cemetery. He hopped off and tethered his mount at a wooden gate. Cyrus respectfully took off his hat as he stalked from grave to grave with a roving eye. After some time, he found Mark DeClaire's name carved onto a simple wooden marker, along with the date of his death—July 9th, 1872.

Two months ago.

Cyrus' wrinkled blue eyes teared up as he slowly dropped to his left knee and knelt beside the grave. Mark was his only child. He would've been twenty-five soon. He should've been married (with young ones) by now. Instead, his boy was murdered in cold-blood and left to rot under a cheap wooden marker! Cyrus' teary face darkened like the fury of an oncoming storm.

"Come to me boy," he commanded.

The mild winds suddenly rose, lifting eerie clouds of dust around him. Cyrus willed his boy's spirit across the barrier between the world of the living and the world of the dead. In moments, Mark DeClaire's transparent form appeared behind his father. The light-skinned black man was dressed very much like Cyrus—except his suit, gun belt, and hat were all black. Cyrus turned around to regard his son. The young man's handsome face lit up at the sight of his father.

"Hi, Pa."

"This is why I told you to go to California by train," Cyrus whispered as a tear rolled down his right cheek.

For a moment, father and son shared a smile.

"Where've you been, boy?"

"Heaven," Mark replied with a smile. "Stop usin' the black magic and they might even let you in some day."

DeClaire spat to his left and rose.

"Your momma was into redemption and Church and salvation, boy. I was raised in the Old Ways. Wished you had an interest in the voodoo. Might've kept you alive."

Mark shrugged.

"How'd you know I was dead?"

"Felt it in my gut," Cyrus grimly remarked. "I came out here to settle things. With that in mind, who killed you?"

"Let it go, Pa. It was my fault."

DeClaire knew his son was lying. Just like his momma, Mark was no good at it.

"Tell me the truth. All of it. And at the very end, you tell me who killed you. Do that and I might not kill everyone in this goddamned town . . . just to be sure I got the bastard."

The ghost sighed.

Mark knew his old man and what he could do. In the Civil War, Cyrus had worked as a Confederate spy and had used black magic time and again. Anyone who got in his way ended up very dead . . . if they were lucky. After the war, Cyrus became a family man and only used his magicks when the coin was right.

"I rode into town and tried to get a room," Mark began. "But they didn't have any place that accommodated coloreds. So, I figured I'd just get some supplies and camp outside of town for the night. While I was at the store, the bank across the street got robbed while the sheriff and most of his deputies were away. They left some kid with a badge behind. There was some shooting in the bank, the deputy rushed in, and got himself gunned down."

"And you decided to step in?" Cyrus asked, knowing full well that was the case. He always taught his son to help those in need. It was one of the few moral tenets that they shared.

"There were four of 'em—all wearing white sack cloths on their heads. I waited until they left the bank and mounted up. Then I started shooting."

"And they gunned you down?"

Mark looked a bit offended.

"Who taught me how to shoot, Pa?"

"I did," Cyrus grinned.

"I got 'em all," Mark confirmed. "Three were dead before they hit the ground. The fourth one fell off his horse, cursing up a storm. I told him not to go for his gun. He did anyway and I shot him. The townsfolk were actually cheerin' me on."

"You should've gotten the hell out of there," Cyrus growled.

"I would've," Mark ruefully smiled. "But that young deputy was dyin'. I asked about the town doctor. But guess what? He was one of the three people who got shot up in the damned bank! By the time I pulled the bullet out of the deputy and stopped the bleeding, the sheriff and his men came back into town."

"What'd they do?"

"At first, they were thanking me for saving the day. But then they pulled the robbers' hoods off," Mark chuckled and shook his head. "Turns out the last guy I shot was the sheriff's only son!"

"Shit," Cyrus turned toward the town.

"Without a word, the sheriff gunned me down. I didn't bother drawing, 'cause my gun was empty." Mark muttered as he eyed his grave marker with clear distaste. "My only mistake was forgetting to reload. And that's how I ended up here."

Cyrus rose to his full height and put on his hat.

"Kindly explain to me how any of that was your fault?"

Mark didn't say anything.

"This sheriff—did he end up in jail or at the end of a noose?" Cyrus asked, his temper on the rise.

"I don't know, Pa. I'm dead—remember?"

"Well, let me find out."

After saying his good-byes, Cyrus allowed his son to return to his heavenly reward. Then he rode back into town, returned the horse, and headed for the hotel. The grieving father picked up his key and climbed the stairs to his simple little room. Inside, he found that his trunks had been set there for him. The former spy reached into his right boot and pulled out a skeleton key.

With it, he unlocked the top trunk first, which was full of his personal belongings. Among the possessions was his last jug of Jamaican rum. Cyrus uncorked it, took a sip, and then put it back. With a sigh, he locked up the trunk and slid it off to the floor.

Using that very same key, he unlocked the second trunk and eyed his well-packed assortment of voodoo supplies. Some of his ingredients were losing their potency after his many weeks of travel. But none of them were damaged.

Cyrus found what he needed, grabbed a wooden mixing bowl, and started to put the salve together. He used this trick in the war. It would be the best way to avenge his son's murder . . . while keeping his face off a wanted poster.

The former spy worked through the night.

The next morning, Cyrus DeClaire strolled over to the Sheriff's Office. Along the way, he pulled out a small glass bottle. The bottle contained the milk-colored salve. To the casual eye, it looked like a harmless white hand cream. DeClaire poured it on his right hand, corked the bottle, and put it away. He then rubbed his hands together, until it was absorbed into his skin.

Afterward, he walked in with a conniving smile.

Sheriff Lester Young, a gruff-faced man in his mid-50's, looked up from his breakfast. Young regarded Cyrus' clothes instantly pegged him as either a gambler or a swindler. DeClaire sized up the sheriff and the tin star he wore on his flabby chest. Next, Cyrus glanced over at the four deputies, who were playing cards in the corner. The junior lawmen eyed him with curious hostility.

"Looking for something?" Sheriff Young asked.

"Yes," DeClaire replied with a well-practiced Texas accent. He respectfully took off his hat. "Name's Roger Salvai. I'm a bounty hunter. Which one of you is the sheriff?"

"That would be me," Young replied. "You say you're a bounty hunter?"

"Yessir," DeClaire continued to lie, as he offered his hand. "I'm after a wanted criminal, sir. I believe he came through your town."

Intrigued, Young reluctantly shook the old man's oddly-scented hand.

"You got a name?" asked Sheriff Young.

"His name was Mark DeClaire, sir. I heard you shot that nigger dead, some two months back," Cyrus continued. "There was paper on him for a few robberies he pulled last year."

The room went dead-silent. Cyrus saw the sheriff cover up his guilty expression quickly enough. Three of the deputies had their poker faces up. The youngest of them fingered his stomach . . . as if remembering an old wound.

"I don't follow you," one of the older deputies said. "You're here to collect the bounty on a guy who's been dead for two months?"

"Yessir," Cyrus nodded. "I was sort of hopin' you'd let me take his body in. I'd be willing to offer you fine gentlemen half of the reward."

"And how much would that be?" asked another deputy.

"$2,000," Cyrus grinned. "Dead or alive."

The youngest deputy looked sickened by the thought but the other three swapped tempted smiles.

"Get the hell out of here," Young growled.

"Excuse me?"

Young stood up, drew his six-shooter, and aimed it at Cyrus. The Cajun resisted the urge to rely on his quick-draw and blast the murdering bastard down, just on fatherly principle. Instead, he allowed a convincing look of fear to cross his face.

"That boy's stayin' on that hill!' Young bellowed. "And if you lay a finger on that grave, I'll empty this gun into you. Now get out or get carried out!"

Without a word, the ex-spy nodded, put his hat back on, and meekly left. He headed for the hotel, checked out, and had his trunks loaded onto a stagecoach headed west. Frankly, he was a bit curious about California. As Cyrus sat across from a sleeping old woman, he closed his eyes and muttered a brief chant in the Old Tongue.

Sheriff Young sat at his desk with a half-empty bottle of whiskey in one hand and a ready glass in the other. His deputies went back to playing cards. Young wanted to drown the memory of that shameful day and did his damnedest to try. He poured himself a glass—

Then, in an instant, the sheriff's mind and body were snatched up by Cyrus DeClaire.

Without so much as a change in demeanor, the big man stood up. The deputies didn't pay Young any mind until he drew his gun and turned it on them. The youngest deputy, while still seated, saw the motion. He jumped to his feet and went for his own gun. Ever since getting shot, he had been practicing his quick draw.

But Young was still faster.

The sheriff deftly worked the gun with both hands and shot the three older deputies dead before they could react. An instant later, the kid shot Young in the chest four times. The big sheriff fell back into his chair, as surprise crept over his face. He tried to say something. Instead, blood rolled out his mouth as his face went lifeless.

Pleased justice had been done, Cyrus allowed himself an evil grin of satisfaction. Then the voodoo master yawned, pulled his hat down over his eyes, and drifted into a restful sleep.

COME AGAIN?

It took me a while to stop crying.

Thousands of dollars richer, Miles Yarlbrough had just left my office with his hat in hand. The best P.I. in town, he had earned every damned penny. Scanning the stack of photos, typed transcripts, and a loaded flash drive on my desk—I had all the proof I needed that my husband was sleeping around. The bastard was banging some Yale grad on the side, a call girl in New York, and a Japanese stewardess . . . for starters.

I should've been happier. After all, I was a gold digger (in the technical sense). Andre D'Armane's personal net worth was at $459 million dollars, as of last week's financials. By all rights, I could gut him in court and leave the philanthropist humiliated. After all, the only thing my "loving" husband valued more than his wealth and good looks was his sterling reputation. Strangely enough, the press hadn't bothered to dig into the D'Armane family's background.

The D'Armanes made their fortune smuggling drugs out of Quebec. During our wedding, Andre's older brother Bernard threatened to kill me if I ever broke his little brother's heart. When I mentioned the scary asshole's threat, some weeks later, Andre confided in me that I had indeed "married into the mob." Yet, Andre assured me that he had absolutely nothing to do with the family business. I remembered how he kissed me with those perfect lips and promised to protect me.

I believed him.

Well, the funny thing is that Andre ended up breaking my heart. While I did marry him for the money, I fell in love with that piece of shit over our four years of marriage. Andre didn't treat me like a trophy wife. He helped me transition from over-the-hill runway model to entrepreneur. Hell, he even loaned (versus gave) me the startup money for my own modeling agency . . . a fantasy I had all but given up.

In the beginning, I figured that I'd simply be good "arm candy" and give him a few babies. But Andre wouldn't let me abandon my lifelong dream. He stole time from his own interests to help me set mine up. I actually repaid the loan and turned my agency into a profitable enterprise. That's when I realized that I loved him. Anyone who'd do that for a silly, aging bitch from Toledo was just—

I succumbed to my grief and freely sobbed.

Afterward, I picked up the flash drive and slowly rotated it between my fingers. Maybe I should forgive him. Andre had been so good to me. Better than I deserved . . .

I slipped the drive into my computer. Through photo after photo, betrayal after betrayal, my grief slipped away. No wonder Andre was so good in bed. He had more women than JFK. And he was seeing them right under my nose. Were it not for some strange late-night calls made to our home, I never would've known. When I called Yarlbrough, I suspected that Andre might've been in danger—especially with a nitwit brother like Bernard.

The last straw was the footage of Andre banging my therapist on her couch. My blood felt like fire as I grabbed some tissue, dried my tears, and collected my thoughts. Leaning back in my chair, I grabbed an empty notepad and picked up a pen. I scribbled a note to fire my therapist. I also added a reminder to get myself tested. For all I knew, Andre had given me something incurable.

Next, I made a note to send Yarlbrough a bonus check for $50,000 for providing such damning evidence. Then, I scribbled Alvin Normenstein's name down. The sly old lawyer was the preferred choice among my social circle. He loved taking divorce cases to court (where he hadn't lost in nine years).

These spirited notes helped calm my splintered spirit. The bliss was interrupted when my cell phone vibrated along the surface of the antique oak writing desk. The Caller ID read "Andre."

Now wasn't the time for confrontation. I needed to set up my divorce plan and then take him by surprise. Frankly, the sly bastard might weasel out of his just desserts if I tipped my hand. It took some effort for me to bite back the rage. Still, I answered the phone with my sweetest voice.

"Hi sweetheart," I answered through the scowl on my face.

"I'm looking for Helen D'Armane," a gravelly male voice shouted over some loud background noise. Traffic, maybe?

I frowned and wondered who this idiot was. Of course it was "me." It was my cell phone.

"Speaking," I said, leaning back into my chair.
"Who is this?"

"I'm the man in charge," he said with an overabundance of melodrama in his voice. "We've got your husband, Mrs. D'Armane."

"Come again?"

"We've taken your husband. And if you don't want this frog bastard chopped up like . . . like uh . . . like uh. . ."

"Like celery?" I offered, fairly certain that this was some kind of sick, stupid joke.

"Yeah! Celery! If you want your hubby back, alive, you'll pay us $50 million in—"

I didn't hear the rest because I was laughing so hard that I dropped the phone. I cracked up until more tears—of mirth—came out of my eyes. I had to give this prankster a hug if ever I saw him. A good cleansing laugh was just what I needed.

I picked up the cell phone.

"This is for real, lady!" he shouted.

"You're saying that you kidnapped my husband?"

"Yes!" he yelled with exasperation. "And you'll need a bunch of tiny coffins for him if we don't get $50 million in six hours."

I glanced at my watch and noted the time, fine with playing out this silly prank a bit longer.

"It's five o'clock p.m. on a Wednesday," I cleverly replied. "The banks are all closed."

There was a pause on the other end.

"Uh . . . make that six hours after the banks open tomorrow then."

"And how do I know that he's alive?"

"Your husband?"

"Yes," I replied with a patronizing sigh. "How do I know he's not already in pieces?"

"I'm calling you on his cell phone, right?" the kidnapper argued.

"Doesn't mean he's alive," I shrugged, fantasizing about Andre really being kidnapped and killed somehow.

"Good point," the kidnapper admitted. "Hold on."

"Okay," I muttered.

As I waited, I wondered how these pranksters got their hands on Andre's cell phone. While he had a sense of humor, he wasn't one for such nonsense . . .

Then it dawned on me—this was not a joke. A bunch of idiots had managed to kidnap my husband. Andre never traveled with protection and was too flashy with his wealthy. It wouldn't be a stretch to believe some amateur hoods grabbed him with some half-baked scheme. If I didn't pay up, they might kill him.

For a moment, a part of me wanted to help Andre. But then I glanced back at the computer, grabbed the mouse, and clicked through the digital photos from earlier. I stopped at one where Andre and a pair of slutty blondes were playing a naked round of Twister in our bed. My moment of compassionate mercy passed.

I let my mind wander over the possibilities as the minutes went by. My arm started to get tired when I heard a rustling sound on the telephone.

"Helen?!" Andre's voice addressed me from the other end. "Helen! It's me!"

"Are you all right?" I asked, my voice full of well-faked concern.

"Just a little banged up, my love," replied my husband, his perfectly sexy phone voice edged with fear. "They want the money by 3 p.m. tomorrow, in untraceable diamonds, or they'll kill me."

I bit back a giggle, relieved that I didn't have to keep a straight face. Fifty million in diamonds? While we were in New York, that was a pretty damned tall order.

"Where?"

"They'll call you at noon with the details. And no police, my love. Be prepared to deliver it alone."

Like hell I will!

"Of course," I lied. "I love you."

"And I love you –"

The phone was pulled away from him.

"There! He's alive! Now, do what he says and you'll get him back with a pulse. Do you understand?!"

"I understand."

"And no police!"

"No police," I repeated, before covering my mouth. With that, the kidnapper hung up.

Then I burst out laughing.

This had to be the best day of my life! I reached into my purse and pulled out a quarter. While I'd love nothing more than to sit back and leave my husband to these morons, it might come out that I received a ransom call and did nothing (an unforgivable sin amongst the wealthy). Worse, the authorities might think I was involved.

So, I readied the quarter for a toss.

Heads: I'd call the NYPD and try to find as much costume jewelry as possible on short notice. Even with their trigger-happy reputation, I'm sure that the cops could probably save my blue blood of a husband and catch his dimwitted kidnappers.

Tails: I'd call Bernard, who'd probably snort something powdery and show up with a bunch of armed thugs. They'd tear this town apart, looking for Andre, and probably get him killed via friendly fire.

To hell with it—I'll do both.

If Andre somehow survives, then I'll take him for everything he owns.

OUTREACH

Rolly Dwanne sat on a blue park bench and checked his cheap brown watch. The chubby black man looked to be in his late fifties, with a sizable salt-and-pepper Afro. He wore a pair of thick-rimmed black bifocals, which didn't soften the sternness of his "street face." His black coat, gray t-shirt, and blue jeans failed to protect him from the late autumn chill. Though, after spending half his life in and out of prison yards, the weather didn't bother Rolly anymore.

The career criminal wasn't here for the fresh air. He was waiting for Theo Johnson—his latest client—to arrive. The poor guy floated to the top of Rolly's list a few days ago; so much so that he put a few other jobs on hold.

Minutes passed before Rolly looked up and saw Theo head his way. The widower moved with a pronounced limp that forced him to lean on an ebony-colored cane. In his early sixties, Theo was a gaunt shell of his once-proud self. Dressed warmly, Theo nodded to Rolly and then sat beside him on the bench. He fished a white handkerchief from his pocket and wiped it across his runny nose.

"It's funny," Theo said with a pained grin. "I used to love the cold as a kid. Now, it just makes my bones ache."

"I hear you," Rolly replied with a deep voice and a sad smile.

Once upon a time, Theo had a wife named Annette.

Eight years before they met each other, Annette was a mother of two with an abusive first husband named Charlie. When she finally decided to leave Charlie, he lost it. Annette was beaten, raped, and left to die in their basement. Had Annette's younger son not found her in time, Charlie would've had his wish. Naturally, the police were called and evidence collected. Annette pressed charges and Charlie ended up with a fifteen-year sentence.

Annette underwent counseling and moved on. She met Theo, fell in love, and remarried. It could have been a happy ending. But, Charlie was released seven years early, due to a combination of good behavior and budget cuts. Thanks to a bureaucratic oversight, Annette was not informed of her ex-husband's release. Charlie learned where Annette was staying, bought a gun off the street, and drove to their house on Thanksgiving Day.

Dinner was at Theo and Annette's that year. One of the guests unknowingly let Charlie in. Pretending to be a cousin, he made it halfway through the living room before someone recognized him and the screaming started. Charlie drew the gun and shot Theo in the knee. Then, he cornered Annette in the kitchen and put eight bullets into her face and torso. While Charlie made it out of the house, the police caught him a few days later. This time, he got life without parole. But that didn't mean much to Theo or Annette.

Almost three years had passed since the shooting.

"Will you take the job?" Theo asked.

Rolly gauged the hopeful expression in Theo's eyes. The poor man relived the events of that horrible day on a nightly basis. There was only one cure for what ailed him.

"I'm inclined to do it pro bono," Rolly replied.

"No," Theo shook his head, with clear hate in his voice. "I'll pay whatever you want. Just kill him. For her. Please."

"Goes without saying," Rolly smiled as he pulled a slip of blue paper from his coat and handed it over. "The name at the top's the messenger service. Wrap the money up in small bills and send it to that address on the bottom. Be there at the date and time we discussed. The security cameras will be off. And you can't be traced if you don't leave anything behind."

"Gloves and a heavy scarf over my face," Theo nodded. "I remember."

"Once I know that the money's gotten to where it's going, the hit is on. There are no second thoughts. After payment, Charlie's mine."

"How will you kill him?" Theo asked.

It's the one question that nagged Theo since Rolly contacted him out-of-the-blue two weeks ago. The hitman personally approached Theo and offered his services. The honest, God-fearing widower was reluctant—even horrified—at the thought. But when left to ponder it, Theo became more comfortable with the idea.

Still, Charlie was in prison. Obviously, Rolly wasn't. Theo, again, wondered if this was some kind bizarre scam or a police sting of some kind.

"You don't need to know," Rolly replied with a low voice. "And this ain't a con. When that money changes hands, your wife's killer is as good as dead. Or, say the word and I'll do him for free."

Theo looked down at his polished brown dress shoes for a silent moment.

"Just knowing he's dead is a bargain," muttered the widower.

"I agree," Rolly nodded as he rose to his feet and stared down at his client. "One last thing. You never talk about our arrangement—not to your shrink, your kids, or even your God."

Rolly's tone and demeanor clearly conveyed an unspoken threat.

"On my children, I promise."

"Then sleep well, Theo."

The grieving widower was barely out of Rolly's line of sight when Annette Johnson appeared next to the hitman. Her transparent, caramel-skinned ghost stood in the same elegant blue dress she had been murdered in three years ago. Based on the modest graying of her cropped black hair, Rolly guessed that she had been killed in her late 40's.

He could see what drew Theo (and Charlie) to her. It wasn't just the nice figure or her pretty face. There was a power in her eyes: something alluring, good-hearted, and strong. In spite of everything, Annette still held her head up high.

Even death hadn't broken her.

"I wish I could have said something to him," the ghost sadly smiled.

"I know," Rolly sighed.

"Thanks for doing this," Annette replied as she gently kissed him on the cheek.

If Rolly was still alive and of a lighter complexion, she would've seen him blush.

"Well," Annette sighed, as she took one last look around. "I finally get to sleep now."

"Rest well."

Annette hesitated for a moment. Rolly could almost read her thoughts. Most of the ghosts he killed for wanted the same thing.

"You want him to suffer—but you don't want to ask," Rolly offered.

She nodded with a hint of shame on her face.

"It'll be slow," Rolly assured her. "I promise."
Annette nodded again, this time with a grateful smile. Then she faded from view as her soul crossed over. Rolly checked his watch again as a jogger ran through him. The killer could be both visible and solid for up to a few hours at a time. But he was still vulnerable to powerful distractions, like Annette's kiss. While it was a minor downside of being dead, it didn't bother him much.

With a moment of concentration, Rolly solidified again. Then, he continued his stroll and devised interesting ways to make Charlie suffer. As a phantom, Rolly had far more tricks than the typical ghost. Once Rolly walked through the prison walls, he'd start by giving Charlie a simple haunting. Then, he'd suffer little accidents, like getting tripped up or cutting his face while shaving.

Next would come the voices—

As Rolly passed a tree, he glimpsed the spiritual remnant of a handsome businessman in a fancy gray suit. Brown-haired and blue-eyed, the transparent ghost was in his late twenties with a slim build and a meek, "mug me" kind of face. Rolly figured that the poor bastard had his whole life mapped out . . . before this.

Curled up in a fetal position, the ghost huddled against the base of the tree. He trembled with closed eyes, reliving his own death. Ghosts like him, if left undisturbed, could suffer until the end of the world in a never-ending, circular hell. Rolly went spectral, leaned over, and gently shook him.

"Please don't kill me!" he yelped.

"You're already dead, man," Rolly chuckled.

His words shocked the poor spirit into opening his eyes. The ghost looked through his transparent hands and began to cry. Rolly gently took him by the arm and half-dragged him to his feet. The victim's spectral tears fell through the ground.

Once he calmed the ghost down, Rolly would talk business. He'd start off by asking questions about the crime. If the details were sufficient, only then would the hitman take the job.

Oddly enough, some ghosts didn't want to be avenged because they were pure of heart. Once that choice was made, those souls tended to cross over right then and there. For those who wanted revenge, Rolly would track the killer down and confirm his/her role in the murder. Then he'd contact someone who cared about the deceased (like Theo) and offer his services.

His was an odd business.

But one thing this city wasn't short on were folks with grudges—whether they were living or not.

THE INHERITANCE

Rosa Fernandez sat on a tree stump, warmly dressed for the chilly autumn evening. The youngest of six half-siblings, the plump waitress looked up at her father's manor house with an unshakeable sense of foreboding. Under the cloudy Maine sky, it looked very haunted.

A few centuries old, four stories high, and made of age-darkened bricks and mortar, the manor had been transported piece-by-piece from England in the 1920's. Rebuilt here by her great-grandfather, the building and its antique furnishings were easily worth tens of millions. The well-maintained home was surrounded by one hundred acres of manicured lawns, exotic gardens,

and pristine forestland, which only added to its value.
Then there was the half-billion dollars' worth of precious
stones reputedly hidden inside.

That's why the teams were here.

Hugh Nokrum fathered six children—including
Rosa—under various aliases. He went to extreme efforts
to ensure they were each born out of wedlock. For some
mysterious reason, he chose poor, working-class mothers
to impregnate. Once each child was born, Nokrum left
town and covered his tracks well enough to avoid
discovery.

Stranger still, Hugh saw to it that each abandoned
mother miraculously received a six-figure "sweepstakes
prize," equivalent to eighteen years of child support
payments. Rosa's mother blew her allotment on
frivolous things and ended up raising her daughter in
near-poverty. The other five siblings all ended up much
better off.

Reuben Turner became a vascular surgeon.

Naomi Secreo-Thornton ended up a senior projects
director at a bioresearch firm.

Todd Gheter practiced clinical psychiatry.

Rhea Benton worked the friendly skies as a
commercial airline pilot.

And Peter Jurpin was a renowned concert pianist
for the Boston Philharmonic.

When Nokrum died of cancer, some six weeks ago,
all of his children were notified and asked to assemble
here on this exact date. Upon meeting for the first time,
they received a tour of the estate and were informed of
the inheritance provision in their father's will. Nokrum's
lawyer, Anthony Murgathol, explained that each of them
would have one million dollars wired to their respective
checking accounts by the end of the next business day.

Then Murgathol gave them two options.

They could take the money and move on with their lives. In doing so, they would forfeit any future claim to the multi-billion-dollar Nokrum family fortune: corporate holdings, real estate, stocks, et cetera. Or, with their million dollars, any of the siblings could assemble a team of experts and search the house.

Five hundred million dollars' worth of precious stones had been strategically hidden within the mansion. Any sibling who wanted a claim to the inheritance had to personally lead his/her team on a search for the stones. Each team would then be randomly assigned its own sector to explore, one day prior. Once inside, they had from sundown to sunrise to conduct a search for the stones.

Then the lawyer explained to the heirs that their late father had a knack for inventing "dangerous toys" in his day. The mansion was full of his finest booby traps. Most of them were linked to a central data server, which was located somewhere within the estate. The traps would be activated one-by-one and in random sequence. The intricate traps would only go off if tripped. Still, as the night went on, the level of danger would exponentially increase. By dawn, anyone still inside would have—in Murgathol's opinion—absolutely no chance of survival.

Murgathol added that anyone who went in could exit at any time and keep whatever valuables they found . . . but forfeit their claim to anything else. Whichever heir made it out alive, after sunrise, and with the most jewels in his/her possession, would be awarded the remainder of Nokrum's estate.

Todd asked why their father hadn't just left his fortune to them in his will, especially since he didn't bother to raise any of them. With a tight smile, the lawyer explained that Hugh Nokrum despised the notion of inherited wealth. He believed fortunes should be earned, not given.

Murgathol then argued that each of them could walk away with one million dollars. Given a bit of time and prudent investments, that money could be turned into true wealth. But inside that mansion was the opportunity to earn billions . . . in one night. In the late Mr. Nokrum's opinion, Murgathol explained, that kind of money should only go to someone bold enough to take it.

Now, exactly thirty days later, the other five siblings had arrived with their teams on a cold Friday evening. Rosa showed up alone and told the lawyer that she had no interest in competing. Her greedy siblings all agreed that she was nuts.

Although they each came prepared for a scavenger hunt of the manor, Nokrum's other children didn't believe the part about the lethal booby traps. Each heir had at least six people as backup, with Naomi having the most people (twelve) on her team. They were going in with weapons, tools, and detailed maps of their respective sectors.

At five minutes to sunset, Murgathol gave the go-ahead to enter the manor house through the main entrance. The lawyer had a red tent set up on the front lawn and invited Rosa to wait along with him. Two uniformed medics and a well-dressed manservant also waited in the heated tent, which contained a small stash of medical supplies and assorted refreshments. As the last of the five teams entered, Murgathol pulled out an ovular remote control. With the press of a button, he activated the mansion's server and the game commenced.

Then, the lawyer asked Rosa why she had come in the first place. She told him that she had taken a portion of her payout and researched her father. Apparently, her father was once considered the best trap master in modern times. Hugh Nokrum designed highly lethal booby-traps for governments, drug cartels, and anyone else who needed to protect their valuables/secrets. Murgathol put on his best poker face as she spoke. Rosa was equally intrigued by her father's deep and abiding interest in the occult. In his youth, Nokrum traveled the world as something of a grave robber. His knowledge of bypassing booby traps had saved his skin time and again in his thirst for occult knowledge. And, while they were given that tour of the manor house, Rosa couldn't help but notice the assorted hieroglyphs stylishly carved into the ceilings and walls. Something of a doodler, she put a few images down on paper and had them examined. The images were a mixture of Mayan and Egyptian incantations of a sacrificial nature. The experts she hired could not quite agree on their significance.

As a result, Rosa decided to show up and see what would happen.

Somewhere around the half-hour mark, a burning male body crashed through a second-floor window. The corpse hit the ground, riddled with multiple arrow-length projectiles. Murgathol consulted a map and figured that the deceased was either Peter or someone on his team. As the night progressed, they heard screams and the occasional explosion from inside the manor.

Sustained by Murgathol's fine coffee, Rosa wondered if anyone would make it out.

During the final hour of the night, two team members exited the mansion through different first-floor windows and only a few minutes apart. One was a member of Rhea's team. The other was a member of Todd's. Utterly terrified, both men were covered with assorted cuts and bruises. After the medics tended to their injuries and provided them each a pill for their nerves, Rosa asked them what happened.

The survivor from Todd's team, a former marine demo expert, poured himself a stiff drink as he went first. By his account, they encountered traps at every turn. About an hour into the search, Todd was sliced in half by a huge pendulum (hidden in the ceiling). Scared by the gruesome death, his former employees decided to abandon the search and backtracked through the traps they had already bypassed. The problem was that they ran into new traps that they had missed the first time through.

In the end, he was the only survivor.

Then Rhea's surviving team member—a retired archaeologist—recounted his nightmarish experience of running into a string of traps as well. They tried to talk Rhea into leaving but she stubbornly ignored them. Then, two hours into the search, she had fallen through a section of the floor, down to her waist.

While the deadfall trap was only three feet deep, it was half-filled with hundreds of scorpions. By the time they managed to get her out, she had been repeatedly stung. They left her corpse behind and simply tried to find the nearest way out. The windows and doors were surrounded by ingenious traps, which slaughtered everyone else on the team.

Neither group found a single jewel.

Murgathol promised to generously compensate them for their troubles . . . once they signed a non-disclosure agreement. The would-be treasure hunters regarded the lawyer with suspicion for a moment and then reluctantly agreed. As the sun emerged, Rosa asked Murgathol if he thought anyone else was still alive in there. The lawyer merely shook his head as he pulled out the remote and disarmed the security system.

Oddly enough, the front doors of the manor house swung open fifteen minutes after daybreak. A thin man with a nice black suit emerged. While Rosa had not attended his funeral, she did see a few old photos of Hugh Nokrum. Unless he had another unknown son, the man exiting the manor house was indeed her father . . . in his mid-thirties?!

As if on cue, the medics and manservant whipped out silenced pistols and gunned down the two wounded survivors. Then they turned their weapons on Rosa, who glared at Murgathol as she raised her hands. The lawyer merely gave her a smug grin and signaled the gunmen to hold their fire.

Hale and hearty, Nokrum shook hands with Murgathol and thanked him for making the necessary arrangements. The billionaire then turned to Rosa and gave her a fatherly hug. She asked him what had just happened. During his travels, Nokrum explained that he had learned of a way to cheat Death.

All that was required was a voluntary sacrifice of sufficient size—say, three offspring. Hence, the large number of illegitimate children. Hugh explained that he didn't raise any of his kids for fear of becoming attached.

So, he concocted this plan and retained Murgathol—an old school chum—to enact it. Murgathol handled everything to perfection: from bringing the siblings together to having Nokrum's body placed in the sub-basement ritual vault. Ironically, he found Reuben's corpse just outside of the vault door. The clever lad had almost avoided the acid traps.

With the deaths of those five siblings, their combined life energies not only raised Hugh Nokrum from the dead but (much to his surprise) made him roughly thirty years younger. The billionaire figured that the two extra siblings were responsible for his renewed youth. Frankly, he was disappointed that so many of his children were foolish enough to participate in such a dangerous endeavor.

Rosa asked him if there were really any precious stones in that death trap of a mansion. With a laugh, Nokrum admitted that they were all tucked away inside of a wall within the main foyer—just past the front doors! It was a neutral sector of the mansion that no one had bothered to search. Each team rushed right by them, eager to get to their respective areas and begin the treasure hunt.

Rosa asked her father what would happen next.

He explained that Murgathol would discreetly collect his liquid assets. Then Nokrum would get a facelift, run off with his wealth, and live comfortably abroad. A fresh crop of heirs was already growing up, ready to be lured in for a rainy day. All he had to do was design a new deathtrap.

Nokrum gave Rosa a peck on the forehead and confessed his pride that at least one of his children was worthy enough to bear his genes. But unfortunately, she'd have to die. With a cocky smile, he left the tent to bask in the warm fall morning.

As her father gloated, Rosa asked him what Hell was like.

Nokrum's smile abruptly vanished as he remembered his afterlife all too well. His troubled expression shifted to one of anger as he ordered Murgathol's goons to kill his eldest child. The trio of shooters stepped out of the tent, raised their pistols . . . and then died as eighteen silenced shots ripped through them from a distant tree line.

Murgathol dove to the ground with surprising speed.

Nokrum turned and ran for the front entrance.

Rosa lifted a dainty left wrist to her face and pointed at her father with her right index finger. Strapped under her blouse's left sleeve was a small radio.

"Take him," she commanded.

Blood erupted from the back of Nokrum's neck from a well-placed round. The wealthy occultist fell over dead (again), his face a mask of shock and pain. From the manicured lawn, Murgathol could only gawk up at her.

"I guess I did bring my own team," Rosa admitted as she gestured for Murgathol to rise. "I wasn't sure what would happen. But I figured I'd want some 'experts' of my own on standby, so I could keep my options open."

With an aching scowl, Murgathol stood. Then he brushed a few lawn clippings from his suit and took a few moments to compose himself. He had advised Nokrum to hire perimeter security for this function but Nokrum refused, convinced that the fewer witnesses involved, the better.

"What would've happened if one of your siblings won the competition?" asked the lawyer.

"They would've been 'jacked," Rosa grinned. "We'd take the stones. And they'd get the multi-billion-dollar estate."

"That would've been . . . fair," Murgathol conceded with a forced smile.

"Give me your cell phone and the remote to the mansion's trap grid," Rosa ordered.

Murgathol handed them over. The heir chuckled to herself as she checked her watch.

"What now?" the lawyer asked with a slight quiver in his tone.

"Now, you work for me, Mr. Murgathol," Rosa snapped as she pulled a small vial of clear liquid from her coat.

"What is that?"

"Poison," she replied. "It takes eight hours to kick in. You won't feel any symptoms to slow you down so you'll have plenty of time to sign everything over to me. Come through and you'll get the antidote and a hefty check. Try anything and you'll die slowly . . . followed by your wife and three lovely daughters. Any questions?"

"No ma'am," Murgathol replied as he took the poison and nervously swallowed it down.

THE MIDDLEMAN

Reggie Hufnick was on his white toilet, suffering the ill effects of a submarine sandwich consumed only an hour before his bedtime. In his late fifties, the pajama-wearing salesman groaned as sweat beaded on his grayish-brown hairline. Reggie eyed his yellow-walled bathroom and decided (right then and there) to paint it some other color in the near future.

That's when he heard the doorbell ring . . . and ring again . . . and again. Around the sixth ring, Reggie glanced at his watch and wondered who needed him at three in the morning. For a moment, he thought about trying to answer it . . . but then his bowels erupted yet again.

Screw it, he thought. *Lorain can answer it!*

After the fifteenth or so ring, he could hear the cursing of his wife as she approached.

"Who's ringing the damn doorbell at this hour?!"
Lorain asked through the closed door.

"Beats me," Reggie replied with a roll of his eyes.

"I'll go see," she yawned.

He shook his head as Lorain's footfalls faded with distance. Once again, Reggie reminded himself that he married her for three reasons: her looks, her ability to cook, and her family's money.

Brains weren't part of the package.

A year older than Reggie, her looks and sex drive both left the building some fifteen years back. These days, whenever he got lonely, his hot young secretary more than satisfied his urges. When he started his marketing firm, Reggie did need her family's money. But after thirty years of wheeling and dealing, he had carved his own little niche in the world. Frankly, he only kept Lorain around because a divorce would cost too much and she could still grill a mean steak—

His thoughts were interrupted by a loud banging noise downstairs, the type that just didn't sound right.

"Lorain?" Reggie called out.

No answer.

"Lorain?" he called out again, more out of annoyance than worry.

Heavy footfalls headed upstairs and toward the bathroom.

Worry lines creased Reggie's brow a half-second before the door was kicked inward. In strode a man with a sawed-down shotgun. He wore blue jeans and a white wife-beater tee, which he filled with a well-muscled frame. His exposed arms and shoulders were covered with old claw and bite marks. Strangest of all was that the man's face was heavily bandaged, from his curly black hair down to his chin. Only his blue eyes, nostrils, and mouth were visible.

"W-Who the hell are you?!"

"One of your satisfied customers," the intruder growled with a raspy Texas accent. "You can call me Ryan. Now wrap it up!"

Minutes later, Reggie lay hogtied behind his two-story house. Facedown in the grass, he had given up trying to slip out of the well-knotted ropes. Lorain and Ryan were in the kitchen for some odd reason. Reggie rolled onto his left side, looked up at the starry sky, and figured that he and his wife were going to die tonight. What bothered him was that he didn't know why. Reggie had made enemies during his years in the mail-order biz, but not any who'd want him dead enough to do anything about it.

Well, if this maniac was going to kill them, he couldn't have picked a better spot. Their house sat smack dab in the middle of nothing but trees and Lorain's modest vegetable garden. The nearest neighbors were a half-mile away in any direction. Even if they heard the shots and called the sheriff, it would be way too late.

Reggie's nose picked up the sweet scent of Lorain's secret-recipe blueberry muffins. It's what she cooked best—even better than her steaks. *Why the hell was this psycho making her cook up a batch of muffins?!* The question weighed on his mind for a long while as nighttime bugs flew over him, drawn by the house's rear lighting.

Eventually, Ryan shoved Lorain outside. Terrified, she carried a plate of muffins in her trembling hands. Still in her nightgown and robe, dried tears streaked both sides of her face. The intruder walked over to Reggie and knelt down with the shotgun casually slung over his right shoulder. With a malicious grin, he looked up at Lorain.

"Damn! You sure as hell can cook, Mrs. Hufnick," Reggie said. "Those muffins smell good enough to die for."

Too scared to speak, Loretta could only manage a terrified smile.

"Figured out what this is about yet, Mr. Hufnick?" Ryan asked.

"No," Reggie replied with a shake of his head. "In fact, I'm pretty sure you're terrorizing the wrong family!"

The masked man laughed a slow, eerie laugh. Reggie wondered what had happened to his face.

"Let's get down to this evening's festivities."

Ryan reached into his jeans and pulled out a small red bottle of *Thinflex* diet pills. Then, he crouched down low, so that Reggie could see the label via the distant kitchen lights.

"Remember these?"

Reggie nodded.

About five years back, he did some business with a small West Coast company that wanted to import organic diet pills from China. Reggie set up a mail-order campaign for them to promote the product. But the product sold less than a week before the company went out of business, all due to a product recall.

"I didn't make the pills, mister! I'm just a goddamned middleman!" Reggie pleaded. "Give me soap, rubbers, or inflatable ducks and I'll sell 'em! That's what I do."

"So, you never heard about what these pills did?"

Reggie shook his head, honestly baffled.

"Know what, Mrs. Hufnick?" Ryan chuckled in her direction. "I actually believe your husband."

A bit of hope crept onto Lorain's wrinkled face.

"In spite of your fly-by-night reputation, it makes sense that you wouldn't be in the know. I'll tell you what: you get a chance to live tonight."

Reggie cringed as the intruder turned toward his wife.

"But your missus here won't be so lucky."

The salesman really didn't love his wife. But something compelled him to speak up for her.

"Why? Why does she have to die?"

"Because I'm in an eye-for-an-eye kinda' mood, Mr. Hufnick," Ryan scowled. "See, once upon a time, I was a handsome guy. I was a musician with a good singing voice and a bright future. My agent tells me to lose my love handles and he can make me a star. So, I hit the gym like a maniac. But I loved my wife's cooking so much that it just wouldn't come off. Then I heard about these diet pills and about how there was a free-trial sample pack."

"So? You had an allergic reaction? Is that what happened to your face?"

The intruder gave Reggie a long, ominous glare. For a moment, he thought Ryan was going to go back on his promise and kill him right then and there.

"No, sir. You're about to see what happened to my face—and why my family's dead."

Ryan took out a little red pill, put the bottle back into his pocket, and walked over to Lorain, who pleadingly shook her head.

"Please don't do this!" Reggie shouted. "She's a good woman. She doesn't deserve this!"

"Neither did my Maggie," the ex-singer quietly said. "Open up, Mrs. Hufnick."

Lorain was too terrified to move. Ryan one-handedly placed the barrel of the shotgun up under her chin.

"Please ma'am: open up."

Lorain closed her eyes and opened her mouth. The intruder stuck the pill on her dry tongue.

"Swallow it," he commanded.

Lorain forced it down.

"Now, these babies work pretty quickly," Ryan continued. "How do I know that? Because I went all the way to China and made the creator try one. Poor bastard ended up worse than me."

"What do they do?" Lorain shuddered.

"Well, they don't suppress your appetite," he replied with an odd smile. "At least, not directly. Eat a muffin."

Lorain's right hand visibly shook as she picked up a muffin and held it in front of her mouth. At the last instant, the poor woman froze.

"Eat it!" Ryan yelled.

Lorain dropped the plate, startled by the abrupt command. But that single muffin stayed in her other hand.

She took a bite.

And another.

And another.

Soon, the muffin was gone.

"You might want to run now, Mrs. Hufnick," Ryan cautioned as he walked over to Reggie.

"Why?" Lorain asked, utterly terrified. "You gonna kill me?"

"Nope," he replied with a sad nod past her shoulder. "But they might."

Lorain spun around and saw nothing. Reggie curiously looked up at Ryan as he slowly dropped to one knee and assumed a shooter's stance.

"Run!" Reggie yelled.

"But I don't see—" she began.

"Just shut up and run!" Reggie yelled louder.

Lorain started to run. A half-second later, a pair of black wolves appeared exactly where she had been standing. Each one was five feet high and looked around with glowing red eyes. They growled at the two men and started to move their way.

"Shoot 'em!" Reggie yelled.

"When it's over," Ryan grimly replied.

The wolves closed in on them. A fleeing Lorain tripped over something in the dark and let out a yelp of pain. Both beasts instantly turned toward the sound, caught the scent of muffins, and then roared with a primal fury as they gave chase. It took the mere seconds to run her down. Reggie closed his eyes as the beasts tore his wife apart under the pale moonlight.

"I stuck to my diet those first few days," Ryan quietly said, still in his shooter's stance as the wolves fed on Lorain's corpse with an unnatural efficiency. "But I passed by a Burger King one day and took home one little Whopper. My wife was about six months pregnant with our first kid—a boy. I took one bite and out they came—those same two wolves. Luckily, we had a lot of knives in the kitchen. But my wife and son didn't make it."

The wolves reduced Lorain to blood and random chunks in under a minute. Then they turned and raced toward the men, full of hunger and menace. With unflinching ease, Ryan gunned down both wolves. The beasts dissipated into black mist as they each took a slug to the head. Reggie quivered in fear.

"T-That's not possible!"

"Oh it is, Mr. Hufnick," Ryan frowned as he rose to his full height. "And guess what? Even though I took that damned pill five years ago, the stuff's still in my system. I can't eat anything but fruit and veggies. The wolves will pop out if I have one little breath mint or the tiniest sip of beer. If I go a week without working out, there's a fifty-fifty chance those damned wolves will come out of thin air. That's why I'm in such great shape right now."

Reggie simply looked up at the sky as tears formed in his eyes. The Texan knelt down and sympathetically patted Reggie on the back as he laid the shotgun down on the wet grass. With practiced ease, he pulled out his bottle again, produced another pill, and gently grabbed Reggie by the chin.

"What are you doing?!" Reggie yelled as he futilely struggled. "You said you wouldn't kill me!"

"The way I see it," Ryan replied, "this will make us even. You could stand to lose a few pounds anyway, Mr. Hufnick. Of course, if you'd prefer, I could always whip out my pocketknife and carve up your face and throat. That way, we can tell everyone we're related. But I *might* nick an artery and you *might* bleed to death. Or better still, I can bite into a muffin and leave you out here to die."

Ryan dangled the little red pill in front of Reggie's fear-filled eyes.

"So, 'Mr. Middleman': what's it going to be?"

THE CONVERT

Frank Grainer slowly came to in cold darkness.

He was naked and bound spread-eagle to a slab of rough-hewn stone. Dried blood matted his brown hair, a souvenir from the recent blow he took to the back of his skull. Stoutly-built and well-muscled, the ex-sailor tried to recollect his recent past. The last thing Frank remembered was his twenty-sixth birthday party. Cecily and her friends had arranged it last-minute. While she wasn't his girlfriend, Frank was working on changing that.

His motives were straightforward.

Cecily was twenty-four, tall, and had the body of a Perfect 10 model. Yet, for some mysterious reason, she didn't realize how gorgeous she was. Instead of using her looks to get her way, Cecily would use straight-up reason. Intelligent and well-read (without being snobby about it), she was a delight to debate and talk with . . . about pretty much anything.

All of these were valid reasons for Frank to be attracted to her. The most important one was that he hadn't been laid since he left the Navy, some three months back. While he could've gone out and banged any number of co-eds at his college, he wanted Cecily to end his dry spell. Right before they met, she had just parted with her last boyfriend and admitted that she was feeling a bit lonely. While Frank knew of a few other guys vying for her time, he was determined to be next in line.

Frank knew that Cecily was starting to let her guard down at the party. If he had pressed his luck just right, he could've gotten a piece of that—

Wait a minute! Frank rolled his eyes. *I'm about to die and all I can think about is sex?!*

He strained to move but couldn't free any of his limbs. He considered shouting for help but changed his mind. Odds were that the only people who'd hear him were the ones who took him. The more time he had before . . . whatever, the better.

Frank tried to think of a good option. Maybe he'd play possum or try to talk his way out of this—nah. This didn't make sense. He couldn't think of any enemies he had made: either as a mess hall cook on a destroyer or as a photography major at Kent State. While Frank hoped

that this was some kind of sick prank, the ex-sailor knew
he wasn't that lucky.
    With nothing else to do but wait, Frank's thoughts
returned to Cecily . . .

He was tapping his G.I. Bill, state college style.
    One day, as Frank rushed to class, he spotted some
fine-assed young ladies playing Frisbee. One of them
was Cecily. Frank landed eyes on her and ignored the
rest. He missed all of his classes that day, just trying to
get to know her better. The topic of a relationship was
never discussed, which both annoyed and attracted him
at the same time.
    Cecily had to have known that he liked her from the
start. Was she playing hard-to-get? Or maybe she was
just that shy? It wouldn't have surprised him, seeing as
she was so religious. Cecily hung out with some folks
from the Church of Active Salvation. While they
claimed to be "non-denominational," they didn't actively
strive to pick up new members or speak in tongues like
other "non-denoms" he had run across.
    The head guy—Reverend Isaac Pasineur—was a
short man with an unassuming face, a few wrinkles, and
the voice of a televangelist. But he didn't have his own
show or a ton of money. Plus, he always wore denim
and plaid, which suited his down-to-Earth demeanor.
The few times Frank attended one of Pasineur's sermons,
he was struck by the pastor's way of doing things.
    The reverend didn't preach, except on holy days.
Nor did he even mention the Bible. Pasineur's style was
to create a congregation that went out and did some
good. That made a lot more sense than sitting in
uncomfortable pews for an hour or two each week. He

liked to say that performing an act of kindness was just as instructional as a sermon.

Every Sunday morning, the eighty-plus congregation would meet in a converted store front church and eat breakfast. Then he'd invite anyone present to come up and tell everyone what deeds they did that week—good or bad—and what they learned from them. The weirdest thing was that Pasineur never took collections or accepted a thin dime from his congregation.

Frank was impressed by the testimonials he heard. These folks donated food, money, and clothes directly to the homeless. They tutored inner city kids. They befriended wounded vets at the local VA. The list was endless.

Cecily had tried to talk Frank into joining.

While he was a man of faith, Frank wasn't a fan of any religion—no matter how cool it looked on the surface. The veteran simply hoped that God knew that he was a good (albeit horny) man and could accept the fact that he preferred to sleep in on Sundays. While he wasn't out to rack up good deeds by the bushel, Frank figured that his moral slate was pretty clean. Whenever Cecily probed for his views on religion, he'd simply change the subject, afraid that his views would ruin things between them—

Wait, he thought.

One moment, he was partying with a bunch of religious folks. Now he was chained up and naked on a sacrificial altar? His fear began to morph into something else. Frank's blood boiled at the possibility that Pasineur—and maybe even Cecily—had set him up. Maybe they would just brainwash him into their little "cult." Or maybe they would just kill him like a sacrificial lamb.

Someone flipped a switch and a blinding cone of white light shined directly upon Frank. He looked around, hoping to confirm his suspicions about Pasineur. But more than ten feet beyond the light, it was utterly dark. The lighting made Frank almost feel like he was on some kind of perverted stage.

"Oh shit!" Frank whispered as he lifted his head and eyed the rectangular stone altar. Some eight feet long and five feet wide, it was covered with dried blood. As he realized that others had been bled out on this thing, Frank struggled against his rope bonds again.

"Please relax, Mr. Grainer," a deep male voice called out from the darkness. "It'll all be over soon."

"What'll be over soon?" Frank shouted back as he stopped struggling.

A black-robed figure stepped into the light with a huge hood over his head that left only his cruel mouth exposed. Frank guessed that his captor was about 6'5", with broad shoulders and a large red urn in his black-gloved hands.

"Your life, Mr. Grainer," said the robed cultist. "Your life."

"Who are you?!"

"I'm but a humble servant, here to do my Lord's bidding."

"Why don't you let me out of here, give me back my clothes, and I'll toss a few hundred bucks into your communion plate? How about that?"

The robed cultist's mouth twisted into an amused grin.

"I don't think we're referring to the same 'Lord,' Mr. Grainer. But don't worry. In a very short while, you'll be one of us."

The cultist pulled the top off of the ceramic urn and began to chant. Frank half-shrieked as a torrent of swirling red energy erupted from it, like water through a high-pressure hose. He watched, horrified, as the energy arced toward the room's high ceiling and then descended directly into his bare chest like a waterfall. Frank suddenly felt frigid, as if he had been dumped into a bath tub full of ice water. He defiantly struggled against his bonds, wishing to God he had never met that scheming bitch—

A nearby wall exploded with such force that it knocked the robed cultist backward. The blast also knocked the urn from his grasp, which hit the floor and shattered. Pasineur charged into the room as the torrent of red energy collapsed. The coldness faded as Frank began to feel somewhat normal again. Then he looked over at Pasineur and his jaw dropped.

The guy was an angel!

The reverend wore his trademark plaid shirt and blue jeans. But Pasineur's fiery-white halo, large white wings, and gleaming metal shortsword gave him away. The harmless-looking old "pastor" ran ten feet to the altar and jumped over it with an eerie grace. Unhindered by his wings, Pasineur landed next to the hooded cultist on the floor. With a powerful right-handed thrust, the angel plunged the shortsword through the evil bastard's heart.

Frank watched with disgust as black ichor gushed from the wound and splashed across Pasineur's face. The head cultist's body writhed in agony for a few moments . . . and then went very still. The grim-faced angel pulled back the hood. Underneath was the pale, horribly scarred face of a man in his late thirties. The cultist's eyes were sewn shut with what looked to be silvery wire.

The angel spun about as other cultists shouted from all around them. Concealed by the darkness, Frank couldn't see them or understand the language they were shouting in. All he knew was that they sounded pissed. Even Pasineur looked worried as he gave Frank a quick glance.

"Are you all right?"

"Yeah," Frank nodded. "Cut me loose!"

Pasineur started to do so when he abruptly spun to his left and parried a pair of crossbow bolts with his sword. Four robed cultists rushed out of the darkness with black long swords. With zealous fury, they attacked Pasineur, who calmly ended each of their lives with swift strokes of his blade. Then, he deftly turned and sliced through the rope on Frank's left hand.

"Who are these guys?!" Frank asked as he turned to his bound right hand and tried to untie the intricate knots that bound him.

"Servitors of the demon Q'alrugaar," Pasineur explained as he spun about and barely ducked under a well-thrown dagger. His face a mask of ire, the angel chopped down two more sword-wielding cultists.

"Why do they want me?" Frank yelled, unable to loosen the knot.

"They want you to kill Cecily," Pasineur grimly responded.

"What?!" Frank glanced over in shock.

Without turning to face him, Pasineur swung his blade three times in Frank's direction. The ex-sailor blinked in awe as he found his other bonds neatly severed.

"Go!" the angel yelled. "Follow the sewer until it dead-ends at a ladder. My truck is across the street!"

Frank rolled off the altar but was too freaked-out to leave. They wanted Cecily dead and he wanted to know why.

"Why do they want her dead?!" asked the vet.

"Get out of here!" shouted the angel.

"Not 'til you tell me why," Frank stubbornly replied.

Truly distracted, Pasineur started to answer, then his left hand abruptly caught a crossbow bolt—mere millimeters from his throat. He cast it aside and kept his back to Frank.

"Cecily's a pure soul—destined to do great things in this world," the angel explained as four more cultists rushed out at him with their strange black blades.

"What? Like Mother Theresa?"

"No," Pasineur grunted as he killed all four of them with brutal efficiency. "She's destined to become the next Reservoir. Now go!"

The term "Reservoir" danced in Frank's mind like a freshly-minted nightmare. His head suddenly pounding, Frank closed his eyes and saw past Reservoirs in action—mortals destined to house the souls of humanity's heroes. Each Reservoir fought evil wherever he/she found it, no matter how great or small. As great scholars, rulers, warriors, artists, and others died throughout history, their accumulated knowledge and life energy flowed into whoever was the Reservoir at the time.

Frank realized that a sort of mystical "baton pass" took place. The souls passed from one Reservoir to the next, making them stronger with each generation. A Reservoir's main weakness was that he/she could only tap into a tiny fraction of that collective power. Still, it made them superhuman when they needed to be.

He (somehow) knew that the last Reservoir would wield it all during the Apocalypse. That final champion would lead humanity against the coming darkness with the combined might, will, and wisdom of humanity's finest. But should the Reservoirs' line of succession break, humanity's fate would collapse.

And the darkness would triumph.

The Reservoirs foresaw their deaths and had dreams that would guide them to their successors. Cecily's predecessor was looking for her. Worse, these cultists had empowered a mortal champion—Frank—to kill her before she could accept the mantle of Reservoir. Frank saw the face of the current Reservoir, a scarred man in his mid-forties with a huge build and a salt-and-pepper crew cut. The ex-sailor felt an instinctive hatred of the man . . . and of Cecily.

Ten cultists rushed Pasineur at once.

This time, the angel had a real fight on his hands. Frank eyed the exit and then Pasineur, who had looked over Cecily since she was born. Once she became the next Reservoir, he would return to Heaven and she'd be on her own. Frank wanted to kill Pasineur too—

No.

Had the angel not stepped in, Frank would've become some demon's willing assassin and killed the woman he . . . loved? The realization distracted Frank just long enough for a cultist to rush him from the shadows barehanded. But Frank Granier had been in enough bar fights to handle one unarmed opponent. He hit the cultist in the jaw with a right cross. It was his standard "fight ender" that he had used in a half-dozen brawls.

To Frank's surprise, his blow knocked the cultist ten feet away . . . minus six of his teeth. The ex-sailor flexed his fingers, which didn't hurt at all. Then, his glance drifted toward the shattered urn and a cold dread went through him.

Pasineur roared in angry pain as he took a wound to his sword arm and dropped his blade. Frank noticed that those ten attackers had been reduced to five. Light-green ichor splashed from the angel's wound as he ducked under a cultist's blade. Wings tucked in, Pasineur and rolled sideways over the altar. With his back to the hole in the wall, he clamped his left hand over the wound and backed up next to Frank. The remaining five cultists rushed over the altar with battle cries and overconfidence.

Pasineur gut-kicked the nearest cultist hard enough to send him flying into three of his pals. They collided into the altar and then hit the floor. But Pasineur didn't see the fifth cultist, who charged him with maddened glee and an axe—

—only to get blindsided by Frank.

Even though the cultist was fifty pounds heavier, the ex-sailor one-handedly grabbed him by the throat and snapped his neck with disturbing ease. Then he dropped the corpse and picked up the axe.

"Thanks," the angel grinned in Frank's direction. "Let's get out of here!"

The mortal needed to tell Pasineur about the urn and the dark energy. To warn him of the evil thoughts in his head . . . or his growing urge to bury the axe into Pasineur's skull. But he didn't want to.

That's when Frank knew what he had to do.

"I can't, Padre."

"Come on!" Pasineur yelled. "We're almost out of time!"

"I'm turning, Padre. Whatever they did to me, you didn't stop it in time."

Pasineur narrowed his eyes and gave Frank a thorough stare.

"Your aura looks untouched," the angel argued. "I interrupted the ritual! I got here in time!"

With a smirk, Frank grabbed the body of cultist he had just killed. Then, with his weak hand, he effortlessly flung it over twenty feet away. As it disappeared into the darkness, Pasineur's jaw dropped.

"No," Frank growled, "you didn't."

The wounded angel eyed the axe in Frank's right hand and backed up a step.

"You left her alone," he scolded through gritted teeth, as true darkness pressed in upon his soul from all sides. "Shouldn't have done that. Find her and run, Padre. Tell her to run fast and run far—'cause I'm coming for her!"

The angel regarded Frank for a sad moment. Then he fled through the hole in the wall. Frank breathed heavily as he turned and waited for the next group of cultists to attack. He didn't know how many were left. But for Cecily's sake, he'd kill as many as he could before he turned.

Suddenly, the lead cultist gasped as he returned from the dead. Slowly, painfully, the big man rose to his feet. Even though blood still oozed from his chest wound, he pulled the hood back over his ruined face . . . and smiled.

"Come on, motherfucker!" Frank defiantly yelled. "You don't have my soul yet!"

"You have a point," the cultist replied. He glanced down at the shattered urn and uttered a word of magic. The object's pieces reformed as it flew into his waiting hands. Frank knew what would happen next and charged in with axe raised high.

Another dozen cultists rushed from the darkness. Frank wasn't as good in a fight as Pasineur. He only killed four before the rest could subdue him. Pinned to the floor, the ex-sailor yelled and cursed as the head cultist opened the urn and resumed his chanting. Once again, red energy erupted from the urn, arced upward, and then down into his chest.

As he felt the cold evil consume him, Frank still hoped that he'd fail in his quest to kill Cecily. Somehow, he knew that Pasineur would keep her alive long enough to become the next Reservoir. She'd be able to defend herself, even against him. It simply wouldn't matter though. Frank would track her down wherever she ran, however it long it took, and in spite of anything that got in his way.

He could only hope that she'd find the will to put him down when that time came.

THE WAKE

Jenny Sagry deserved a full house tonight.

Barely seventeen, she lay in a brown coffin lined in white satin. Peacefully arranged in death, she wore a black gown, with her small hands placed across her flat stomach. Her raven-black hair was cut short and neat. Her tiny face was just perfect. The mortician had done an awesome job on Jenny, to the point where she almost looked alive and sleeping.

I choked back a sob and wiped a tear away as I took in the standing-room funeral home crowd. Every high school clique was represented: from the Goth-type weirdoes she hung around with to the dumb jocks she tutored (like me). Half the town also showed up to pay their respects. Even Sheriff Graye and some of his deputies attended, all in ceremonial uniform. Jenny's family had lived in Merden Falls since before the Civil War and they were always well-regarded. When one of their own tragically died, the community came together to mourn.

Her immediate relatives took up the front rows. There were her parents, who held hands and whispered back and forth. Kate (her sister) bounced her infant daughter on her lap, in the hopes that the kid wouldn't scream her head off at some key moment. Behind them were cousins, aunts, and uncles—all forlorn at the loss of the finest gal alive. Reverend Metche walked passed me and headed for the podium in front. The tall, balding pastor paused at Jenny's coffin and stared down at her with clear sadness in his eyes.

Then he said a few kind words over Jenny and how he remembered the day he baptized her. She was about five years old. Reverend Metche smiled as he recalled that her first words, after being baptized, were: "Towel, please." That drew a few sobbing chuckles from those present.

He mentioned her many bright points, from being an honor student to giving her time to various charitable endeavors. After a quick prayer for her soul, Reverend Metche offered up the podium to anyone who wanted to say a few words. Kate handed the kid to her parents and went first. A line of people formed along the wall, all eager to say their good-byes.

I was tempted to get into that line, too. But I couldn't. No words would come to me and I'd just make a fool of myself. Then, Mina Schamm entered through a side entrance, dressed in bright colors, like it was a party. At least she wasn't wearing that over-sweetened bug repellent she called perfume. Male eyes hungrily followed her as she pardoned herself my way. Literally the ditzy cheerleader, Mina wore a fake expression of sadness as she took me by the arm and kissed me on the right cheek.

"Hi," Mina said with a fragile smile.

I simply grunted in reply and turned my eyes forward. While she was arguably the hottest woman in town, I dumped Mina without regret. For the last month or so, she had been trying to get back together with me. It was driving me nuts. Normally, I'd just pull my arm away and tell Mina to fuck off (yet again). But this wasn't the time or place for that.

What she didn't know was that I dumped her for Jenny Sagry. Such a choice wasn't my style. I used to value body and tongue skills over character and integrity. Jenny changed my entire outlook. Back when she was tutoring me into a C+ in Spanish, it was like Cupid walked up behind me with a sledgehammer and took my head off. I couldn't get Jenny out of my mind. Being around her was like being high. I wasn't very good at being subtle, so she caught on quickly enough. It turned out that Jenny had a crush on me since the fourth grade. Somewhere along the way, her crush had become something more. While she wasn't too keen on dating me behind Mina's back, we gave it a shot.

The sneaking around added spice to things, I think. Her friends didn't know. My friends didn't know. And Mina was too busy picturing herself as my future wife to notice. Jesus! We hadn't even graduated from high school and Mina was already talking about honeymoon locations. All the while, I faked being a loyal boyfriend . . . while spending as much time as I could with the only woman I'd ever love. Being the angel she was, Jenny told me that she couldn't keep seeing me on the down-low. She told me I had to make a choice between her or Mina.

An hour later, I dumped Mina.

Had I not lost my cell phone (again), I'd have done it right then and there. It felt great. I didn't tell Mina the real reason for the breakup (that I was madly in love with my Goth chick tutor-slash-dream girl). I simply gave Mina other relevant reasons—like I had outgrown her goofy ass. I wasn't lying about that either. My brief time with Jenny had raised my standards to the point where Mina was just too boring to know.

Jenny and I got tighter and tighter. We agreed to wait a few more weeks before we started publicly dating. Those eighteen days were amazing.

We never argued.

We'd finish each other's sentences.

We were really in love.

Then, nine days ago, some drunken asshole stole a pickup truck from a class party. Jenny was walking home late when . . .

I heard she wasn't killed on impact. That she landed in a ditch and might've died in slow agony, alone and afraid. They found the pickup on the side of the road the next day. Whoever stole it ran out of gas and just abandoned it with a bunch of empty beer cans inside.

Sheriff Graye personally led the investigation. Apparently, they had no leads, suspects, or a chance in hell of finding the coward who killed my first love. I could feel the blood rush to my face at the thought of Jenny's killer walking free—possibly in this very room.

Kate stepped down from the podium, unable to continue through her tears. I glanced over at Mina and was annoyed that she was still latched on to my right arm. As folks took turns remembering Jenny's many good deeds, Scott came up on my left, dressed in a gray suit and black tie. Short and freckly, he was a decent punter and a much better friend.

He gave Mina a shy smile and then held up my cell phone. I lost it again, a few days before Jenny died. When I couldn't find it, I ended up getting a new one.

"Thanks," I whispered as I used the excuse to pull my arm away from Mina and powered up my phone.

I always turned it off when I wasn't using it . . . a habit I picked up while dating Mina. She'd love to call me out of the blue and waste my time talking about nothing for way too long. By the time I started sneaking around with Jenny, Mina was used to not being able to reach me.

"Where was it?" I asked.

"A janitor found it in the workout room, behind one of the leg machines."

"Must've fallen out of my gym bag," I shrugged as I started to pull up my old messages—

Then I glanced over at Mina and remembered that Jenny used to call me up, too. She'd say something short, smart, and sweet—and then hang up. Mina didn't need to know about Jenny and me. I guess no one else did either. Some selfish part of me hoped that she had left me some messages. At least I'd have that soft voice to remember her by.

"Excuse me," I muttered as I stepped away from Scott and Mina.

It took me a few minutes to make my way to the nearest door. As I passed my fellow mourners, I noticed that Jenny left me three messages . . . one of them from the night she was killed. My heart kicked into eighth gear as I rushed outside and entered my pass code.

"Sam," Jenny's sobbing voice called out to me. "Sam . . . I don't want you to worry. I called 9-1-1. They're on their way right now. You'll get the [coughing] whole story. I just . . . if anything happens to me, just know that I love you."

Her voice got fainter.

"From the moment I laid eyes on . . ."

Then silence.

Tears flowed as I waited for her to say something else—anything else. The message ended and gave me the option of saving it. I wiped my eyes as I did—

"Give me the phone, son," Sheriff Graye's gravelly voice gently ordered from behind me.

What. The. Fuck?!

I turned around to find the barrel-chested sheriff standing just outside of arm's reach. Even though he was about forty-seven, he looked ten years older right now. I took in his thinning black hair, rugged face, and guilty eyes. Since I was a little boy, I knew Sheriff Graye. Trusted him. I wanted to be like him some day. Now, he held out his left hand. His right hand was on his hip holster, which was unclasped. In it was his huge .357 revolver. I grew up hearing about Sheriff Graye's skill with that gun and how his dad (a former lawman) had taught him how speed-draw and shoot like the cowboys of old. But right then, I didn't give a fuck.

"Give me the phone, Sam."

I raised the phone, looked down at it, and then up at him. Then I slipped it into my right pocket as angry questions jumped into my head. I figured I would ask a few and see if he was dumb enough to talk.

"Did you kill her?"

"Of course not!" Graye replied. "But that phone's evidence. Now hand it here."

"Who killed her, Sheriff? You're protecting somebody. Who?"

His reaction gave it away. Graye was too used to being on the high ground to have much of a poker face.

"Whoever killed Jenny was at a high school party, Sheriff," I said. "Who was it? Your daughters aren't even ten, so it wasn't them. And you wouldn't cover up for just anyone's kid."

"Give me the phone," Graye repeated, looking around. No one was outside. It was too damned cold and windy. Even the limo drivers were inside. It was just us. But the longer this bore out, the more likely there'd be witnesses.

"She called 9-1-1, you motherfucker!" I growled at him with trembling rage. "Jenny asked for help and you left her to die on the side of the road!"

My grief and my rage were line dancing in my skull. I didn't care about Graye or his gun or anything else. I just had to know why. Graye cocked his head, surprised by my reaction to Jenny's death. Then he glanced over at the funeral home.

"I thought you were dating Mina."

"*You thought wrong!*"

He sighed with regret. God, I wish I had that gun and five minutes alone with the good sheriff.

"I'm sorry, Sam. Honestly, I am. But this case is closed."

"Fuck that!" I yelled as I stepped right into his face. He was big. So was I. We stood about eye-to-eye. He actually froze up, unable to blast me down or even step back. For all his rep and for all the fear he inspired in the local punks, Sheriff Graye was nothing more than a bitch with a badge.

"She's dead and I love her!" I sobbingly raged. "Not 'loved'! Love! Present tense! She's gone! Now you fucking answer me! Who killed her?!"

Graye looked at me for a cold eternity.

"One of the kids at the party was WITSEC," he finally said.

I looked for a lie in his eyes. There wasn't one. He glanced up at the sky, near tears himself.

"I was closest," Graye confessed. "I floored it and was halfway to the scene when the feds pulled me over. They told me that Jenny was already dead, Sam. They took the records, the suspect, and every shred of evidence—except for that phone. They set the cover-up, not me. I had to go along or some big case of theirs would go up in flames."

I wanted to kill him and he knew it. He looked at the murder in my eyes and shook his head slightly, warning me not to try him. Slowly, I reached into my pocket and dropped my phone at his feet. Graye looked down at it. Then at me. He was too chickenshit to go for it. So I backed away.

"You're not a man," I spat as I turned and walked back to the funeral home.

Graye wouldn't shoot me in the back. There'd be too many questions and not enough rationale. He'd simply get in his car and drive the phone to his fed contact. The feds would go through my messages . . . and realize that I gave Graye my new phone. Halfway up the steps, I heard Graye's cruiser start up. Turning to watch him leave, I pulled my old phone. The one with Jenny's voice on it: my last real link to her.

Like I'd ever part with it.

I stepped inside and realized that people were still speaking about Jenny. Now that I had something to say, I didn't bother to wait in line. Instead, as one of her Goth-chick pals was about to take the podium, I politely cut in front of her.

The crowd murmured and one of Graye's deputies noticed the phone in my hand. The fucker looked scared as he pulled his radio and muttered into it. Jenny's friend was pissed . . . until I whispered what I was about to do. Then she stood back and nodded, shocked as hell. I wiped my last tears away and cleared my throat.

"My name's Sam Fimner. Jenny used to tutor me. But in the end, just before she died, we were dating."

"What?!" I heard Mina yell from the back of the room.

The murmuring got louder. I looked down at Jenny's family.

"On that night, Jenny left me a voicemail. It's the last thing she said before she died."

I held the phone close to the microphone and hit the "Speaker" button. Once they heard Jenny's last message, I'd tell them what Graye told me. Her family would go to the media. The media would go after the feds. The scandal would force this shit out into the open.

And heads would roll.

PROFESSIONAL COURTESY

Cedric Young patiently waited at a graffiti-covered telephone booth under a cloudless night sky. His beige three-piece suit, cream-colored shirt, and matching tie rippled in the night breeze. The polished dress shoes he wore were black with disguised steel tips.

At an even 220 pounds, his 6'1" frame was hard-muscled and covered with old wounds. His face was handsome and expressionless, with a neatly-trimmed goatee and a pearly-white smile that rarely saw the light of day. Aged beyond his thirty-eight years, his brown eyes had a look of "intelligent evil" about them that scared most people. A black mane of braided locks ran halfway down his back.

In his left hand was a briefcase with $13 million in untraceable diamonds—the ransom he had been instructed to bring. The diamonds were a significant part of his nest egg, which he wasn't happy to part with. Cedric checked the time on his platinum Rolex and then glanced over at the phone. Ready and eager to kill someone, he kept his eyes open and waited for it to ring.

Small shops and restaurants lined both sides of the street, all of which were long-since closed for the evening. In the hour he had been waiting, many a pedestrian had strolled by him. Some were working types heading to or from work. Others were local Philly gangbangers who openly admired his evident wealth. While Cedric could've kept a lower profile, the dark-skinned man barely had enough time to pull the ransom together, much less pull a wardrobe change. Besides, he wasn't worried about muggers, having killed so many of them over the years. Snapping back to the moment, Cedric wondered who'd be stupid enough to set a meeting here. There were dozens of more discreet venues, with fewer or no witnesses—

The phone rang. He picked it up.

"That's one of the many things I love about you," Amanda's relieved voice said through the receiver. "You're always early."

Cedric allowed himself a relieved grin.

"You all right?" he asked, suddenly feeling eyes on him . . . and not the bystander variety.

"Bound and blindfolded, but I'm fine," she replied. "You have the goods?"

"Yes."

"Across the street is a dark alley. Walk into it."

Amanda started to say something else. But her captors yanked the phone from her and hung up. Cedric did the same. Then he turned toward the dark alley as a frown inched over his face. It was a great place to get jumped, shanked, and left to bleed out.

Such is death, Cedric thought as he jaywalked across the empty street and into the alley. Once he stepped into the darkness, rough hands grabbed him from both sides and behind. He guessed three men: all large and reeking of clashing colognes and cigarette smoke.

Cedric could've killed them with ease.

Instead, he restrained the urge as a fourth man walked up and thoroughly frisked him. A former assassin, Cedric had hung up his spurs. He was a private investigator now. While he didn't mind hurting people, he no longer took lives. It wasn't because he was haunted by guilt or fears about the consequences. No, he quit out of love. Love for Amanda McConnell—a one-time cat burglar he had once been contracted to "neutralize."

"Goddamn man!" the heavily-accented voice of the fourth man exclaimed, as he found Cedric's third holdout piece. "How much shit you got on you?!"

"Six guns, eight blades, a garrote wire in my Rolex, and a half-pound of Semtex in my left breast pocket," Cedric calmly responded.

He could almost smell their collective fear as he was disarmed. Good. That means they knew his reputation. Sometimes, it made being a detective so much easier. The simple threat of reverting to his old persona kept things civil.

He liked civil.

They took the briefcase. Finally, someone shined a light as they carefully examined its contents. Cedric got a good look at them. They were all Latinos in expensive clothes, with guns sticking out of their pants like only amateurs would. One of them stuffed the retired assassin's toys into a white cloth sack.

They weren't locals. The accent of the man who spoke was Colombian, maybe? Cedric weighed the short list of people stupid enough to snatch his lady—foreign and domestic.

Ernesto Cervantes topped that list.

Eight years back, Cervantes was a rising underboss in a Colombian drug cartel. Then, he killed a batch of undercover DEA agents who had almost infiltrated his outfit. Such a coup would have been seen as a "win" for any aspiring crimelord . . . had one of the dead agents not been Amanda's godfather.

Back then, Amanda was one of the best thieves in the game. No security system could keep her out. On the rare occasion things went wrong, no prison could hold her. When she heard about her godfather's death, she sent a note to Cervantes' boss that simply read: "Kill Cervantes. Or you lose a plane."

Naturally, her threat went unheeded. So, Amanda hijacked one of the drug lord's cargo planes, which just happened to be full of product. She left a bomb on board, bailed out, and blew it up over the ocean. Then, she sent another note: "Kill Cervantes. Or you lose another plane."

Cedric grinned as he was shoved further down the alley. He loved that story and she loved telling it. Amanda stole and destroyed four more cargo planes—all loaded with drugs and/or cash. All were heavily-guarded by Cervantes' best men. But it just didn't matter. Following each hijacking, Cervantes' boss would receive another note.

Only after the fifth lost plane did Cervantes' boss take Amanda seriously.

The underboss then found himself marked for death and chose to run. Assassins from all over the world tried to cash in on the seven-figure bounty on Cervantes' head. Cedric was busy with a French client or he would've joined in the hunt. As fate would have it, Cervantes eluded multiple near-deaths and managed to fall off the grid . . . until tonight.

If it was Cervantes, Cedric would have to kill him. Odds were that Amanda wouldn't mind—for her godfather's sake. His only regret would be that he'd be doing the deed for free.

They reached the back door of the *Jade Dragon* Chinese restaurant, which was closed for the evening. While it wasn't the best location, Cedric had to admit it was the last place he'd have looked for her. One of the thugs knocked three times, and the door quickly opened to reveal two more goons. Both triggermen allowed them entry and then followed them inside.

They passed through the otherwise-empty kitchen and over the bodies of two Chinese men—one in his fifties and the other in his late twenties. Probably the owner and his son. Both victims had been bound, gagged, and shot in the head execution-style. Cedric frowned as he was shoved through swinging red doors and into the dining area.

The tables and chairs had been cleared away, which made the crimson carpeting stand out. There was no sign of Amanda. He eyed the white concrete ceiling and bit back a smile.

Ernesto Cervantes sat on a black leather couch, which was placed at the center of the cleared area. The ex-underboss was almost forty-three, with a 5'6" frame and a bulging gut. But he looked closer to fifty, the result of his stressful years on the run. He wore an expensive gray suit, collarless white shirt, and a cocky sneer. An ornate, ivory-tipped walking cane was propped next to him.

His once-average face was heavily-scarred on the left side. Cedric recognized the facial wounds, which were consistent with buckshot from a 12-gauge. He also spotted a deep knife scar on Cervantes' throat, which peeked just over the collar of his fancy white shirt.

Idiot or not, the man was a survivor.

One of Cervantes' men walked over with Cedric's briefcase and opened it for him. The scarred Colombian leaned forward and sniffed the diamonds with a smile—as if someone put a freshly-baked pie under his nose. He then leaned back and imperiously pointed downward. The minion closed the briefcase, set it at Cervantes' feet, and stepped away.

"So," Cervantes said with a damaged, heavily-accented voice. "I finally get to meet the big, bad killer. Hey, you hungry? They were just closing up when we got here. The noodles aren't half-bad."

"Where is she?" Cedric asked with ice in his tone. Still all-smiles, Cervantes gave a nod to another one of his men, who produced a hand radio and muttered something in Spanish.

"She'll be out in a minute," he promised with sincere admiration. "That gives me time to ask you something."

Cedric impatiently folded his arms.

"You were the best, right?" the Colombian began. "Over 500 kills without a single mark ever—and I mean *ever*—getting away. You were Death in a suit! I heard about this time when you . . ."

As Cervantes rambled on and on, Cedric sized up the scarred man's body language and realized he was more than a little high. Considering the nature of his injuries, it made sense that he'd need drugs for the pain . . . and end up addicted to them.

It struck the ex-killer as oddly ironic.

Another pair of well-dressed minions dragged Amanda into the room. At thirty-six years old, Amanda was an athletic, dirty blonde dressed in a blue skirt and white blouse. She limped slightly and her wrists were tied in front of her with thick rope. A blindfold covered her modelesque face and a white cloth gag was tied around her mouth. Aside from the limp and a purplish bruise on her right cheek, Amanda appeared to be unharmed. The muscles in Cedric's jaw clenched as he waited for his opening.

When it came, he'd kill them all.

Cervantes tapped his cane against the carpeted floor and regained Cedric's attention.

"My one question for you is this: why'd you give it up for her? If I had your rep, I'd never quit for a woman, man. Never."

Cedric gave Cervantes a cold smile. "She makes me happy. Now let her go."

Cervantes pretended to think about it. Clearly, he had to kill them both. Amanda's little hijacking spree ruined his ambitions, his face, and his health. And he had to know that Cedric would kill him on general principle.

Cervantes snapped his fingers. Amanda's escorts threw her down. Landing hard, she grunted in pain as his thugs drew their guns and pointed them at Cedric.

"Pull her blindfold and gag," Cervantes snapped, his face all-business now. "I want this bitch to see her man die."

Cedric not only kept his composure but cracked his knuckles and smiled. The triggermen exchanged nervous glances. They knew that a killer like Cedric wouldn't enter such an obvious trap without a way out. Only Cervantes didn't seem worried. Amanda's blindfold was pulled down and her gag removed.

"You all right?" Cedric asked.

"Nothing too serious," Amanda winced as she eyed her left foot. "I twisted my ankle when they came after me."

"Does he have anyone else around?" he asked.

"Nope," Amanda replied with calm certainty. "Just these losers. What now?"

"I'd kill the help," Cedric sighed. "But you made me promise to stop killing people, remember?"

"Oh yeah," Amanda sighed back with a knowing grin. "Let's forget that: just this once."

"You're the best," the retired assassin replied with a sincere smile.

Then, Cedric's eyes narrowed as his gaze swept over the room. With an eerie suddenness, the eight armed triggermen had their guns ripped from their hands, all at the same time. They gawked as an invisible force sent their weapons flying into a neat pile on the floor, just within a few feet of the couch.

Then, all of Cervantes' men were telekinetically slammed up into the ceiling.

Then, to the floor.

Cervantes jumped back onto the couch with a yelp. He was pinned there by the shock and dread of watching his men get slammed back-and-forth between the ceiling and the floor. He stopped counting after the fourth brutal impact. Fifteen seconds (and a few dozen impacts) later, Cedric allowed the eight dead Colombians to fall from the ceiling.

Bits of plaster and concrete fell as Cedric willed a pair of handguns from the pile and into the air.

"H-How'd you do that?!" Cervantes yelled.

Cedric simply scowled in reply as he mentally pointed both guns at Cervantes. Amanda glanced at the ropes that bound her and cleared her throat. Without looking her way, Cedric made them snap apart like thread.

"Want a blindfold, Ernesto?" Amanda teased, still on the floor.

"Please! I can give you money—"

Ya' can't do that if you're dead, Ernesto, Amanda telepathically interrupted.

Cervantes jumped at the sound of her voice in his head.

"You read minds?!"

And then some, Amanda replied.

"What's he worth?" Cedric asked, hoping it was more than his nest egg.

"Two million and change," she said aloud.

"To answer your question: everyone thinks I chose not to kill Amanda," Cedric admitted. "The truth was I couldn't. She 'saw' me coming from a mile away—and decided not to kill me."

"I considered it a professional courtesy," Amanda explained. "You just don't run into a fellow psychic every day: especially a cute one."

Cedric gave her a kissing gesture. Then, he telekinetically tossed both handguns to Cervantes. As the weapons landed in his lap, the Colombian didn't dare move.

"Show him your best trick, honey," Cedric muttered.

Amanda closed her eyes and intensely focused. Cervantes deftly grabbed both guns—but not of his own volition. He strained not to press both weapons against the undersides of his jaw . . . and failed miserably. His thumbs unwillingly cocked the hammers.

"I don't get it!" Cervantes stalled as he vainly tried to move the pistols away from his head. "If you're so damned powerful, then why'd you let my guys kidnap you?!"

"I can read hundreds of minds at once," Amanda confessed. "But I can only toy with two or three at a time, max. With the nine of you, something might've gone wrong. Besides, it looks more believable if Cedric came in, killed all of you, and saved me."

"And you'll make a great example to anyone else thinking of messing with us," Cedric added.

The telekinetic walked over, gently picked Amanda up with both arms, and gave her a quick kiss on the lips. Cervantes began to recite the *Lord's Prayer* in fluent Spanish.

Next to one of Cervantes' thugs was the cloth sack. Cedric lifted it up with his mind, emptied its contents, and then rearmed himself without lifting a finger. Sweating profusely, Cervantes repeated the prayer while desperately trying to move. Given half a chance, he'd have shot them both. But Amanda's grip on his mind was ironclad.

"Damn!" Amanda exclaimed. "How many guns did you bring?"

"Don't start," Cedric muttered.

"Did you bring any Semtex?"

The tube-shaped Semtex charge floated in the air in front of them.

"Of course," Cedric replied. "But I don't think I'm gonna use it this time."

"Why not?" Amanda frowned. "I thought you liked blowing up messy crime scenes with a lot of bodies."

"Yeah," the telekinetic shrugged. "But this is a family business—with two of the family members dead in the kitchen. Seems kind of wrong to shred their livelihood."

Amanda frowned at the damaged ceiling and didn't envy them their remodeling bill. She'd arrange for some kind of discreet compensation for their next of kin.

"Besides, once the cops gather up the evidence, we'll just come back and snatch anything incriminating," Cedric finished.

"I'm rubbing off on you," Amanda purred as she snuggled against him, proud of the man he had become.

Cedric made a scoffing sound as he fondly took in the murder scene one last time, satisfied that he hadn't lost his touch. He then willed his diamond-filled briefcase into Amanda's hands. The Semtex charge floated into his right trouser pocket.

"Okay," Cedric playfully sighed, "you've got my diamonds. I've got you."

The ex-assassin sighed with mock distress.

"Y'know, I feel like we're forgetting something," he teased.

Cedric and Amanda exchanged smug glances. Then they both glared over at Cervantes, who was still praying.

Amanda pursed her lips. "I think you're right."

Just as Cervantes finished reciting the prayer, yet again, he heard Amanda's voice in his mind: *This is for my godfather.*

Cervantes' scream of terror was cut short by a pair of simultaneous gunshots.

THE END

ABOUT THE AUTHOR

Marcus V. Calvert is a native of Detroit who grew up with an addiction to sci-fi that just wouldn't go away.

His goal's to tell unique, twisted stories that people will be reading long after he's gone. For him, the name and the fame aren't important. Only the stories matter.

You can find his books on Amazon. Also, you can follow him on Facebook and/or Patreon.

Website: **https://squareup.com/store/TANSOM**

Facebook: **https://www.facebook.com/TalesUnlimited**

Patreon: **https://www.patreon.com/IVillain**

Made in the USA
Middletown, DE
02 June 2019